THE CROWN JEWEL MYSTERY

THE SHERLOCK HOLMES AND LUCY JAMES MYSTERIES

The Last Moriarty
The Wilhelm Conspiracy
Remember, Remember

Upcoming:
The Jubilee Problem
Death at the Diogenes Club
The Return of the Ripper

The series page at Amazon:
http://amzn.to/2s9U2jW

OTHER TITLES BY ANNA ELLIOTT

The Pride and Prejudice Chronicles:
Georgiana Darcy's Diary
Pemberly to Waterloo
Kitty Bennet's Diary

Sense and Sensibility Mysteries:
Margaret Dashwood's Diary

The Twilight of Avalon Series:
Dawn of Avalon
The Witch Queen's Secret
Twilight of Avalon
Dark Moon of Avalon
Sunrise of Avalon

The Susanna and the Spy Series:
Susanna and the Spy
London Calling

OTHER TITLES BY CHARLES VELEY

Novels:
Play to Live
Night Whispers
Children of the Dark

Nonfiction:
Catching Up

THE CROWN JEWEL MYSTERY

A SHERLOCK HOLMES | LUCY JAMES STORY

BY ANNA ELLIOTT AND CHARLES VELEY

Typesetting by FormattingExperts.com
Cover design by Todd A. Johnson

ISBN: 978-0-9991191-0-5

1. FROM THE NOTES
OF JOHN H. WATSON, M.D.

Sherlock Holmes stood motionless beside me, watching intently as Mrs. Palfrey struggled with the lock to her son's bedroom door. Holmes was plainly impatient, but he said nothing, for none of us wished to add to the poor woman's obvious distress. Her plump hands shook, and she was weeping.

Finally, the lock clicked, the knob turned, and the door swung open to reveal a barren, cramped space containing two narrow beds and little else by way of furnishings. Neither bed appeared to have been slept in.

I caught a faintly acrid scent on the cold air coming from the single open window and saw a pair of faded yellow curtains fluttering in the morning breeze. The time was just after nine o'clock, and the date was Monday, October 28, 1895. Holmes and I had left Baker Street in haste before daybreak to meet Inspector Gregson and his men. At the inspector's telephoned summons, we had foregone breakfast to make the two-mile journey to Mrs. Palfrey's rooming house, a stolid brick four-story structure on Great Ormond Street.

Now, what we had come to investigate was immediately apparent. On the floor between the two beds, huddled against the wall beneath the window, lay the crumpled remains of Simon Palfrey. He was still fully dressed.

Holmes took three swift strides and stood beside the body, but he did not examine it. Rather, he appeared to be watching the street outside, although he stayed behind the curtains and well away from the window.

Mrs. Palfrey waited in the doorway, plainly unwilling to advance further.

Gregson, florid-faced and Nordic in appearance, addressed her in a kindly tone. "Please tell us what happened, Mrs. Palfrey."

She had not yet caught her breath from climbing the stairs and was still trying to control her sorrow, dabbing at her reddened eyes with a small handkerchief. Finally she spoke. "It were six o'clock, and he would have been late for work. I knocked at the door. He'd locked it. So I let myself in with my own key and there he was—"

"Have you moved him?"

"I touched his forehead. It was cold. I locked the door and telephoned the police straightaway."

"Were you in the habit of waking your son on workdays?"

"Sadly, yes. For the past few months."

"Why?"

"He had taken to keeping late hours. And drinking."

"Where?"

"Mostly at the Swan. It's only a few blocks from here so he can manage to walk home safely even after a ... late evening. He has pills he takes to clear his head, and he is generally all right in the morning—though that comes all too soon, I'm afraid, what with the hours he's been keeping."

"Pills?"

"He showed them to me. Said they'd done him a power of good."

Holmes had been standing back from the window, but looking out of it quite frequently from time to time. Now he knelt beside the dead man. I noticed that Simon Palfrey was dark haired and bearded with a neatly trimmed goatee.

Holmes pulled a small pasteboard box from the man's waistcoat pocket and held it up.

"Oh, that's them," said Mrs. Palfrey. "Coca lozenges. His nerve tonic, he called it."

Holmes opened the box and sniffed the contents. "We will have these analyzed," he said, tucking them into his jacket pocket.

"Do they smell funny?"

"They smell perfectly ordinary. But we must eliminate the possibility that they contained the poison that appears to have killed him. Did he take one last night?"

"I don't know. He didn't say one way or the other. I was waiting up for him, like always, and he just looked in on me and said goodnight, and then he went upstairs. And that's the last—"

She broke off and pressed her handkerchief to her eyes once again.

"If I may, Mrs. Palfrey," Gregson said. "Just one more question. When you telephoned the Yard, you gave the desk sergeant the name of the establishment where your son was employed. Would you kindly verify that for us now?"

"He is—*was*—a clerk at the Capital and Counties Bank on Oxford Street. It's a mile away. It takes him about twenty minutes to walk it. I came to wake him at six so that he would get there on time this morning."

Capital and Counties was the bank where Holmes kept his accounts. It was also somehow connected with Gregson's call to us and with Holmes's sense of urgency as we hurried here this morning. Holmes and the Yard no doubt had a reason for taking a particular interest in the bank, but as yet Holmes had not shared that reason with me. It was one of his most annoying habits, keeping his plans secret until the last possible moment.

Gregson continued. "And I believe you told the desk constable that your other son is also employed at Capital and Counties?"

"Yes. Jeremy is a guard there."

"At this moment?"

"He works nights. He gets off at seven. Jeremy generally takes the Turkish bath after his shift. For his health."

"And he shares—beg pardon, shared—the room with Simon."

"It's quieter on the top floor so they both can sleep undisturbed. And we need the better rooms for the paying lodgers." At that moment there came the sound of heavy footsteps on the stairs.

"That'll be Jeremy now," said Mrs. Palfrey.

She was proven correct as a short, ruddy-faced. clean-shaven man of about thirty years pushed past the constable and entered the room. His face and hands were flushed, likely from the effects of the Turkish bath, though his breathing was normal. His features bore a striking resemblance to those of the dead man, with the same dark hair, wide forehead, and high cheekbones. Had he not been clean shaven, the resemblance would have been even more striking.

Mrs. Palfrey broke the news just as the new arrival caught sight of his brother's body. His eyes widened in shock, and his limbs seemed to lose their strength. He sat down heavily at the foot of one of the two beds and buried his face in his hands.

After giving Jeremy a few moments to recover, Gregson made the introductions. He did not name either Holmes or myself, referring to us as two gentlemen who sometimes render assistance to Scotland Yard.

Jeremy appeared not to notice us, nor to care about our presence. He sat head downcast, nodding and rocking slowly from side to side. Finally he spoke.

"He said he was givin' up them pills."

"Where did he get them?" Gregson asked.

"Some gal he was sweet on. She—they would go out drinking after work. Not that he could afford it. I kept tellin' him she was no good and that the life of a boozer was no good and that people at the bank were startin' to talk. He wouldn't listen."

Holmes asked, "How long had this been going on?"

"Couple months. Six weeks, maybe."

"Yet you thought he was going to reform?"

"I kept telling him he ought to try the Turkish baths after work instead of goin' to the pub. Do something *con*structive for your health, I tells him, not something *de*structive. I thought I'd finally got through to him, because two Saturdays ago we were both off from work and he took me up on it. Afterwards he said the visit to the baths had done him a world of good. He said he could scarcely *believe* how much good it had done him. But then he went straight back to his old ways. Drinkin' and wastin' his time with that woman. That's what we had the row about yesterday. I knew what he was up to because he'd stopped makin' up his bed again. I'd come home, and it would be all rumpled and smellin' like a gin mill."

Holmes nodded. Then he said, "Might I ask you a favor, Mr. Palfrey. Would you please turn out your pockets?"

Though appearing momentarily surprised, the man complied without hesitation. Holmes went through the items, naming each in succession as he lifted it up. "A wallet with a few bills and a card identifying you as an employee of the Capital and Counties Bank. A pocket handkerchief, slightly damp. A small key ring with four keys. This one is to your front door, is it not? And this is to your room—the room you share here? And the third, this smaller one?"

"Oh, that is to my locker at the bath. And the other is to my locker at the bank, where I keep my uniform."

Holmes turned to Gregson. "We must leave here at once," he said. "There is not a moment to lose."

2. FROM THE DIARY
OF LUCY JAMES

"So what do you think?"

I turned to study the young man beside me. John D. Rockefeller Jr.—Johnny, as he was known to his friends—was in his early twenties and handsome, with dark hair and a clean-shaven, sensitive face.

He was impeccably dressed in a dark suit, tan overcoat, and shining black top hat, with a white silk scarf around his neck to ward off London's damp autumn chill.

I raised an eyebrow. "I think that was the least romantic proposal in the entire history of marriage."

Johnny's mouth curved in a quick grin. "In my defense, it is the tenth time I've asked you."

"Exactly. Surely a tenth proposal ought to be marked by something more momentous than a *what do you think?* Fireworks or hot-air balloons at the very least. Now, focus."

I looked up at the tall, stone-built building before us, my heart quickening.

Johnny gave me a martyred look. "You know, most people arriving in London for the first time want to see Buckingham Palace ... the Tower ... London Bridge. Not a dreary branch of the Capital and Counties Bank."

I ignored him.

I hadn't even been in London a full day, but I liked what I had seen very much: the old half-timbered buildings sandwiched in amongst the more modern ones, the sleek black hansom cabs, and the streets filled with people from all walks of life—from wigged members of Parliament, hurrying to meetings in the House of Lords to organ-grinders and orange vendors and Italian acrobats performing on street corners.

I even loved the slightly yellow-tinted fog that crawled, phantom-like, along the cobbled streets and narrow lanes.

At some point, I intended to see all the sights of the great city, though my list of places I wanted to visit was somewhat different from Johnny's: the original site of Shakespeare's Globe Theater ... the Poet's corner in Westminster Abbey ... The Lyceum Theater, where Ellen Terry was currently playing Queen Guinevere in Henry Irving's production of *King Arthur*.

For the moment, though, there was absolutely nothing more important to me in the world than getting inside the Oxford Street branch of the Capital and Counties Bank.

"We need to find out who the bank manager is in there and get him to see us," I said.

Johnny waved a dismissive hand. "That's easily done."

That was probably true. The Rockefeller name alone was enough to allow Johnny easy access almost anywhere he wished to go. If past experience were any guide, all he would have to do inside the bank was introduce himself, and the bank manager would start tripping over his own feet to carry out Johnny's lightest wish.

"Thank you for coming with me," I said.

Johnny smiled. "Anything for you, Lucy James."

My heart tightened again. Lucy James was the name I'd had for my entire life. As I looked up at the bank, though, my nerves felt stretched, my pulse racing with the thought that I might—possibly—be about to discover where the name had come from.

We walked up the steps, Johnny introduced himself to the doorman on guard at the door, and—true to expectations—we were rapidly ushered into the inner office of the bank manager, whose name—according to the brass plaque on his door—was Mr. Albert Poole.

"Mr. Rockefeller." Mr. Poole greeted Johnny with an outstretched hand and a beaming, if slightly anxious, smile.

He was a middle-aged man with a rotund figure, reddish-brown hair parted exactly in the middle of his forehead, and quite possibly the most perfectly trimmed toothbrush mustache I had ever seen. Silver-framed spectacles perched on the end of his nose.

"This is a great honor, a great honor, to be sure," he went on. "I have never had the pleasure of meeting your father, though of course I know him by reputation, and you may be assured that we at the Capital and Counties Bank stand ready to assist both you and him in any way that we possibly can."

He sat behind a large, mahogany desk that was bare of even the slightest trace of clutter. Papers were neatly stacked in labeled trays: *incoming* and *outgoing*. His sheet of blotting paper was clean and new and perfectly aligned with the desk corners. Even his pens stood ramrod straight in their holders.

"Thank you." Johnny gave Mr. Poole a friendly smile. It was one of the nicest aspects of his character; despite his family background, he had somehow managed to grow to adulthood without becoming in any way spoiled or thinking that the world existed to do his bidding.

He dropped into one of the two leather-upholstered chairs in front of Mr. Poole's desk. I sat down in the other.

"Actually what I require isn't for myself, though. This is my friend, Miss Lucy James." Johnny nodded, indicating me.

Remaining quietly in the background wasn't exactly a strength of mine. But in this case, I kept strictly silent, letting Johnny perform the introductions.

I could see my own faint, wavering reflection in the glass that covered the bookcase behind Mr. Poole's desk: dark brown hair beneath the brim of my flower-trimmed brown straw hat, dark-lashed green eyes, pale oval face.

I could *also* see a long row of filing cabinets next to the bookcase, where presumably Mr. Poole kept his records—records that might finally give me some clue as to where I *got* my dark hair and green eyes.

"Miss James is newly arrived in London," Johnny went on. "She is to join the D'Oyly Carte Opera Company at the Savoy Theater and requires a bank account to be opened here in London, where she may deposit her salary and all of that sort of thing."

Mr. Poole's face fell. Even the squared-off corners of his mustache seemed to droop.

"If you could just—" Johnny began.

I kicked his ankle.

"Ow!—I mean, ah!" Johnny shot me an aggrieved look, but correctly interpreted my message. "Actually, now that I come to think of it, it would be convenient for me to open an account here in London, as well," he said. "I'm not sure how long I'll be over here for, but it would be good to have an account I could use for writing checks or draw on for ready cash."

Mr. Poole immediately brightened, rubbing his hands together. "Certainly, Mr. Rockefeller, certainly! I would be only too pleased. And you, as well, Miss James, of course."

He gave me a polite nod. I couldn't entirely blame him for not viewing my business in quite the same light as Johnny's. An as-yet-unknown American actress was not at all the same thing as the young Rockefeller heir.

"I have some blank pass-books here, if you wouldn't mind filling them out with your names and addresses? Then you may deposit any money you wish with Mr.—" He stopped, a look of mild annoyance crossing his face. "No, that's right, Mr. Palfrey failed to turn up for work today. You may make any deposits you wish to me, and I will see that they get credited in your accounts."

I took the small, blue-covered booklet he offered, and Johnny did the same.

I filled out, *Lucy James, Savoy Hotel, London* on the front flyleaf.

Then I glanced sideways, giving Johnny a hard look, nodding very slightly towards the file cabinets.

Johnny cleared his throat. "I wonder if ... do you think I might have an ... ah ... that is, a cup of tea?"

I shut my eyes, fighting the urge to bang my forehead against the bank manager's desk.

Mr. Poole looked slightly startled, but nodded. "Certainly, Mr. Rockefeller."

He pressed the bell that sat next to his inkwell and blotting paper, and a moment later a uniformed page boy appeared in the doorway.

"Some tea, Jasper," Mr. Poole said. "Quickly, now."

Jasper was back barely a minute or two later, and Mr. Poole rose from behind his desk and crossed over to the doorway to take the tray from the boy's hands.

"*Tea?*" I hissed in a nearly inaudible whisper to Johnny. "A bank manager doesn't fetch his own tea! We need to get him *out* of the office. Ask to see the bank vaults."

Johnny's eyes widened. "The vaults? I'd feel like an idiot."

"Don't make me kick you again. *Please?*"

"Now then. Cream? Sugar?" Mr. Poole set the tea tray down on the desk in front of us.

Johnny cleared his throat. "Actually, I was wondering whether you might let me have a tour of the bank vaults." He gave a slightly unconvincing laugh. "Want to be sure any money I leave here is entirely secure, you know."

"The vaults?" Mr. Poole looked taken aback, but recovered. "Ah … well, of course, if you wish." He had probably never dealt with someone of Johnny's wealth or social standing before; for all he knew, this was simply how young men of immense fortune operated.

Mr. Poole looked at me. "Miss James, would you like …"

"Oh!" I manufactured a startled, slightly anxious expression. "Oh, no thank you. The vaults must be underground, mustn't they? I think I'd be a little afraid to go down there."

Behind Mr. Poole, I saw Johnny's lips twitch at that.

I smiled into the bank manager's eyes. "I'll be quite all right staying here, if you don't mind."

My heart was thumping, my nerves still coiled tight with the need to hurry, but I forced myself to wait for a count of thirty after Johnny and Mr. Poole left the room. Then I got up, slipped over to the filing cabinets, and took out one of the hairpins from the coiled braid at the nape of my neck.

I'd long ago taught myself to pick locks, and the ones on Mr. Poole's filing cabinets weren't complicated. A few quick twists and I had the first drawer open, though it proved to be the wrong one. The account numbers on the labeled, leather-bound bank ledgers inside were all lower than the one I was looking for.

I took a breath, closed and re-locked the cabinet drawer, and tried again.

On the third try, I found the ledger I wanted. I pulled it out, set it down on Mr. Poole's desk, and started to turn the pages. My pulse beat in sharp, hard bursts, almost blurring my vision.

For my entire life, I'd lived without any idea of who my parents might be, without any idea of whether I even *had* living parents or a family somewhere in the world. My school fees were paid promptly and anonymously, allowing me to attend one of the most exclusive finishing schools for girls in America. Clearly, whoever had made it their task to fund my education had money.

But no one wrote to me, no one visited me ... whoever my anonymous benefactor was, he or she took no personal interest in me at all, as far as I was aware. Even the payments were made anonymously, sent to the school by a mysterious trustee. And despite my persistent questions from the time I could remember, no one at the school would say a word about the trustee's identity or even tell me where his office was located.

Three months ago—using much the same techniques as today—Johnny and I had gained access to the bank in Farmington, Connecticut, where the checks paying my tuition were routed from. Those bank records had given me no names, but I had found an account number with the Capital and Counties Bank, Oxford Street, London.

I'd had no idea then how I was going to get myself across the Atlantic, though I had been prepared to beg, barter, bribe, or do whatever else might be necessary.

But someone from London must have heard me sing at a concert, because not long afterward, a telegram had appeared offering me a job as a soprano in the chorus of the world-famous D'Oyly Carte Company, which was based at the Savoy Theater in London.

Now I was here. On Oxford Street. At the Capital and Counties Bank.

I ran my finger down the row of entries in the bank ledger.

Account number 1368 … 1369 …

Invisible hands wrapped around my chest and squeezed as my finger touched the entry labeled 1401.

I scanned the cramped notation written beside the account number—just as the doorknob to Mr. Poole's office turned.

3. LUCY

I suppressed several bad words that would no doubt shock Mr. Poole if I said them out loud, slammed the ledger book shut, rammed it into the filing drawer, and slid the drawer shut.

No time to lock it.

I dropped back into my chair in front of the desk, just in time to smile at Johnny and Mr. Poole as they came back in.

"How were the vaults? Were they secure enough?" I asked.

"Very impressive." Johnny gave me a questioning look, but I shook my head.

Johnny was a nice young man and a good friend, but not particularly quick at understanding wordless messages. I would need more than just a look to tell him what I needed from him.

"Excellent." Mr. Poole picked up the passbooks we had filled out. "In that case, I will just get these—"

"Johnny also wanted to see the room where you keep the safety deposit boxes," I interrupted. "Wasn't that right?"

Johnny gave me a completely blank look. But then he sighed. "Oh, ah … yes. Of course. My mother has some … ah … old family jewelry. She would need a safe place to store it, just in case she ever comes to London, you understand."

Mr. Poole was apparently becoming used to Johnny's requests by now. Either that or the prospect of storing Rockefeller family valuables was too dazzling to resist. He hardly blinked. "Certainly, Mr. Rockefeller. If you will just step this way?"

This time, I fell into step beside Johnny as Mr. Poole led the way out of the office, away from the bank's main reception room and down a long hallway towards the back. We went through a set of swinging double doors and then past what looked like a meeting room, furnished with a large oblong table and chairs.

"Is there any corner of this blasted place you *aren't* going to make me have a sudden yearning to see?" Johnny muttered.

"Shhh. There was no name on the account number," I whispered back. "But whoever owns the account *does* also have a safety deposit box here. Number 538."

Johnny gave me a look of alarm. "Lucy, you aren't going to—"

"Here we are." Mr. Poole reached a door to the right and drew a bundle of jangling keys from his pocket. "Our night watchman also owns a set of keys to this room in case of emergency, but apart from his, mine are the only keys in existence."

The door was made of metal, rather than wood, with a huge combination lock in the center. Certainly not the kind of thing I would be able to pick with a hairpin.

Mr. Poole spun the wheel three times, inserted a key into the lock's center, and then swung the door open with a flourish, revealing a small, narrow room, lined from floor to ceiling with metal safety deposit boxes.

"Our space here is perhaps small, but I would wager you would not find a more secure space even in the Bank of England itself. In fact"—Mr. Poole straightened his cravat, looking solemn—"well ordinarily, this information would be kept in strictest confidence, but in light of the honor you are doing our bank by conducting business with us, Mr. Rockefeller ... well, without naming names, I may say that your mother's would not be the only important family heirlooms to be entrusted to our deposit boxes here. Only this week, a certain member of the English peerage deposited a necklace here, with a large emerald said to have been worn by Queen Elizabeth I herself."

"Very ... impressive," Johnny said. He shot me a resigned look. "I suppose I want to go inside? Yes, of course I do, why wouldn't I?"

I had a feeling that unlike me, Johnny genuinely wasn't overly fond of closely confined spaces, and the safety deposit room did have a claustrophobic, airless feeling.

I stepped in after him, then turned to Mr. Poole. "Oh, Mr. Poole, I'm so sorry. I nearly forgot to tell you. One of the page boys came to your office while you and Johnny were in the vaults. He said that there was a message for you from your wife? Something about the doctor's visit this morning?"

Mr. Poole's face blanched visibly, anxiety pinching the corners of his mouth. "Dratted boys, can't be bothered to write down a message or see that it's delivered properly." He looked at Johnny. "Mr. Rockefeller, I beg your pardon, would you mind—"

Johnny might not intuitively understand how my thought process worked; in his defense, very few people did. But he *could* take a cue.

"Of course, Mr. Poole. We'll wait here for you. Don't bother yourself, we'll be quite all right."

The bank manager hurried out, his face still anxious.

Johnny faced me with a look that hovered between amusement and disbelief.

"How did you know he has a wife? Much less that he was expecting news from a doctor's visit this morning?"

"He has a wedding photograph of himself and his wife propped up on the bookcase in his office. Her dress looks as though it were fashionable in the mid-1880s, so they've been married about ten years. Mr. Poole is obviously a neat, fastidious man. Look at his office—look at his *mustache*. But this morning, he missed a spot shaving on his chin, which made me think he must be worried about something—probably something at home. It can't be the bank clerk who didn't come to work today. Mr. Poole didn't know about that when he was shaving. Also, when he opened the top drawer of his desk, I saw there was a doctor's bill and a receipt from a druggists' shop for a bottle of cough mixture inside. I think he and his wife must have a child who's ill."

I did feel guilty, though, for trading on Mr. Poole's worry for his son or daughter in order to get him out of the room.

Johnny's look of amused disbelief deepened. "Have you been reading Sherlock Holmes stories again?"

"Not lately."

There hadn't *been* any new Sherlock Holmes stories published—not in the past two years since Dr. Watson had broken the news of Sherlock Holmes' death in *The Final Problem*.

I'd felt that loss almost as keenly as though I had actually known the famous detective, instead of merely reading the stories like thousands of others in copies of *The Strand Magazine*.

Which was clearly ridiculous, but Johnny had it backwards. I wasn't able to deduce Mr. Poole's family background because I read about Sherlock Holmes' detection methods.

I had always, for as long as I could remember, noticed things like photographs and uneven shaving jobs and half-glimpsed doctor's bills. And when, at the age of 12, I had first come across Sherlock Holmes in *A Study in Scarlet*, I had been fascinated, true, but I could also remember the wave of sheer *relief* that had swept through me when I read the account of Holmes rapidly and correctly inferring Dr. Watson's service in Afghanistan, war wounds, and drunken brother.

Finally, I knew that there was at least one other person in the world whose mind worked at least a little like mine. Finally, I wasn't the only one.

I stepped closer to the right-hand wall of deposit boxes, scanning the numbers.

I found number 538 a moment later and took out my hairpin again.

Johnny looked at me in alarm. "You do realize that if anyone catches us, we'll be arrested?"

"They wouldn't dare. You're far too important a personage. At worst, we'll end up with a strong reprimand. Besides, I don't plan on being caught."

I inserted the hairpin into the lock, pressing gently. My fingers were twitching with impatience, but forcing a lock wasn't a process that could be done sloppily or in haste.

Beside me, Johnny gave a theatrical sigh. "I see how it is. You're only interested in me for my fortune and influence. The least you could do is agree to marry me, after that."

I turned the hairpin a little, feeling the lock's tumblers start to shift. "Are we counting this as proposal number eleven? Or … ten and a half?"

The hairpin slipped, and the lock slid back into its original position. *Drat.*

I bit my lip, sweat prickling on my hairline. "Anyway, you can't marry me. Your family would object."

Johnny's family was keen for him to marry a girl back in America, a senator's daughter. It was one of the reasons I didn't take his proposals particularly seriously.

"My family would come around once they met you," Johnny said. "They'd love you. Even my father. You'd be a princess."

That was very close to the literal truth. Johnny's father, John Davison Rockefeller Sr., was by far and away the wealthiest man in America. Johnny, his only son, was as close to royalty as it was possible for an American to come.

I glanced at him sideways and almost sighed.

Maybe there was something wrong with me. Thousands of girls in America would cheerfully commit murder in order to hear the words *will you marry me* coming from Johnny Rockefeller's lips.

Johnny managed the nearly impossible feat of being not only fabulously wealthy, but also handsome—and a genuinely good, decent young man. He was steady, reliable—and he wasn't even a spendthrift, despite the fact that he and his father could probably buy the bank we were standing in and every other building on the street and never even miss the money.

And I looked at him and felt … friendly. I *liked* Johnny. The thought of marriage to him, though—endless society balls and formal banquets and every tiniest detail of one's life being reported in the society pages of all the newspapers—felt like being smothered under a heavy blanket.

I slid the hairpin into the deposit box lock again. Mr. Poole had left the door to the safety deposit room partly ajar. I could hear the low murmur of voices from bank customers in the outer room down the hall as people stepped up to the bank counters and made their deposits or withdrawals.

No approaching footsteps as yet, but I had no way of knowing how long it would take Mr. Poole to discover that he hadn't actually received any messages from home.

Johnny was watching me. "Lucy, have you thought—that is, have you considered that you might not like what you find in there?"

He nodded towards the box.

"Of course I have."

I might not have any firsthand experience with families, only what I had seen on visits to friends' and schoolmates' homes. But what I did know with a chill, bone-deep certainty was that there was no harmless reason, no happy story that ended in my being abandoned as a baby and raised for the past twenty years without any idea of who I really was.

"I'd rather know the truth, though, than be stuck always wondering."

Even if my parents were dead—or simply had never wanted me—I would rather *know*.

I looked up at Johnny. "Thank you for coming with me and for agreeing to help. I really am grateful. No matter what I find out."

Johnny looked sober, but he didn't argue, only watched me in silence a moment more. "I didn't mean that, you know," he said. An unaccustomedly serious, earnest note had slipped into his tone. "About your only caring about my money. Actually, I think you're the only girl I've ever met who genuinely *doesn't* care about—"

"Shhh." I interrupted, putting a hand on his wrist.

Uneasiness was suddenly crawling over my skin, though for a brief instant, I had no idea *why*. There was still no sound of approaching footsteps from outside the door, no—

Realization struck me. There was no sound of *anything* coming from the bank's outer room. The murmurs of voices had gone silent.

I had barely started flipping through possible explanations for what that could mean when a woman's high scream rent the air, followed immediately by a sharp, percussive *boom*.

Johnny gasped. "What on earth—"

"Quiet!" I clamped my hand across his mouth this time.

He went obediently silent, but his eyes—dark and frightened looking—searched mine over the edges of my fingers.

My pulse was beating in my temples, the blood running cold all through my veins. I leaned forward, speaking barely above a whisper.

"I think the bank is being robbed."

4. LUCY

I pressed myself against the wall, just inside the door, straining to listen for any sounds from the bank's main room.

We were too far away for me to hear anything clearly, and there was the swinging set of double doors between us and the lobby, too. But I heard a brief snatch of a man's harsh voice, issuing what sounded like orders to keep still and be silent.

"*Quiet!*"

I caught that word, delivered in a sharp, angry bark.

"What do we do?" Johnny asked. His whisper sounded panicked.

We already knew that the bank robber—or robbers? I couldn't tell whether there was only one voice out there or more than one—was armed. The sound I'd heard before had been a gunshot.

Was anyone hurt out there? Or dead? I had no way of knowing that, either.

I drew a steadying breath, shoving away both shock and fear while ordering myself to think.

"They don't know that we're here," I whispered back. "And there must be some sort of a back entrance to this place. We could try to find it, slip out and find a police—"

Too late.

I cut off speaking, biting my tongue to stop a gasp as a man's figure appeared in the doorway of the safety deposit room.

A masked man, his face obscured by a kind of black hood that left only his eyes visible. He was tall—taller than Johnny—and correspondingly broad. And he was leveling the barrel of a gun directly at us.

"All right, move," he ground out.

He had a deep voice, with an accent that sounded like the ones I'd heard from the dockyard workers when my ship had arrived at the Victoria and Albert Docks yesterday morning.

He jerked the gun in a quick, impatient gesture for us to come out of the room. "Hands where I can see 'em," he grunted.

At the sight of him, I had automatically palmed the hairpin I'd been using to pick the deposit box lock. Now as I raised my hands in front of me, I let the pin slide down into the edge of my jacket sleeve.

A single hairpin against a heavy Webley revolver still didn't give me particularly good odds, but it was better than being entirely unarmed.

Johnny and I stepped back out into the hall. The masked man made a prodding motion with his gun, urging us towards the lobby. "Walk."

I took a last look into the safety deposit room. It probably was a sign of my mental processes being even more peculiar than I'd thought. But at the moment my uppermost feeling wasn't fear of the armed man behind us. It was sheer, boiling anger at being dragged away, just when I was *finally* on the verge of discovering something about myself.

I would probably never get a chance like this one again, not even if Johnny and I came back here on another day. Mr. Poole didn't strike me as an intellectual giant, but he would surely be suspicious if I came up with a *second* ploy to be left alone with the deposit boxes.

The thought made my fingers twitch with the urge to smash something—or wrench the gun away from our masked bank robber and use it to knock him unconscious.

I could do it. He was following too close behind us for safety; whatever else he might be, he was not much of an expert at holding people at gunpoint.

I could see the maneuver play out in my mind's eye: spin, knock his gun hand up with the flat of my palm, kick his leg out from under him, club him over the back of the neck as he went down.

But Johnny kept dropping back, trying to put himself between me and the gunman, which was chivalrous, but also inconvenient. And I couldn't tell him to stop it without also alerting the masked man.

We walked down the hallway, through the double doors, and out into the bank's main lobby. My heart contracted, fear replacing anger in a hard jolt.

The bank clerks and the customers who had been doing business a few moments ago were now seated in a ragged circle in front of the row of counters at the back of the room.

Ten … eleven … I counted thirteen of them. Thirteen people who were now hostages along with Johnny and I.

A hole in the ceiling and a scattering of plaster dust on the floor showed where the gunshot Johnny and I heard had been fired. A warning shot, intended to frighten and intimidate. No one was injured—yet.

I spotted Mr. Poole sitting on the ground between two frightened-looking clerks. The bank manager's face was white as cheese curds, his lips moving as though he were either praying or silently swearing.

One of the bank customers, sitting on the edge of the circle closest to the counters, was a fair-haired woman with a little girl who didn't look as though she could be more than five or six. Both mother and child were sitting rigid, their faces white and terrified. Silent tears had left tracks down the little girl's cheeks, but she was clearly too petrified to make a sound.

Another gunman stood in the center of the room. Like the man who had found us, he was masked in a black hood, but his weapon was a double-barreled shotgun.

"Is anyone else back there?" he demanded as we came in.

His voice was gruff as the other man's, but with an accent that wasn't English. I frowned, trying to place it.

"No," the man behind us grunted. "Just these two."

"Sit down." The second man gestured with the shotgun, motioning for Johnny and I to join the others.

German, that was it. He sounded German. In addition to the hood, he wore black gloves, but there was an inch or so of skin visible between the top of the glove and the cuff of his dark-colored shirt. His wrists were pale, with a light dusting of fair hair.

I swallowed, letting my eyes travel over the rest of the room. Two more men—also hooded, also dressed in black and armed—guarded the doors.

Four armed men that we knew of, and there could be more elsewhere in the building. Not good odds.

I started towards the cowering group of people, the heels of my boots echoing on the marble floor. Johnny followed close behind.

I took a place next to the little girl and smiled at her.

The German speaker and the man who'd found us were talking together in low voices, obviously preoccupied, and the other two men had moved away from the door to circle the room, checking windows to make sure they were both closed and locked.

All were too far away from us to hear.

"What's your name?" I whispered to the child.

She gave me a wide-eyed, frightened look, but then whispered back, "Rosie."

"*Hush*." Her mother caught hold of her daughter's hand in a tight grip, warning her to silence. I supposed I couldn't blame her for not wanting to draw the gunmen's attention.

Although we weren't the only ones of the group to be speaking in low undertones. Two of the men on my other side were carrying on a nearly inaudible conversation, their heads bent to hide the fact that their lips were moving.

"—more of us than there are of them," I heard one murmur.

He was a fair-haired, slightly doughy young man whom I recognized as one of the clerks who'd been waiting on bank customers when Johnny and I arrived. I'd heard one of the other employees use his name in passing.

Barret? Brian? No, Boyd. That was it. One of the other clerks had walked past him and said, "Have the new checks come in yet, Boyd?"

Now Boyd was leaning towards the man directly next to me and speaking in a rapid whisper.

"We need to act now—before they have a chance to do anything worse."

The second man was a solid, ruddy-faced man of perhaps thirty-five, with a determined chin and the look of someone who might have played rugby at school.

I remembered seeing him in the line of customers waiting to be served.

He nodded in answer to Boyd. "I'm in. We go together?"

A chill wrapped around my spine. "That is a supremely bad idea," I murmured.

The two men startled at the sound of my speaking; they'd obviously not realized I was paying any attention.

They exchanged a look, and then Boyd leaned in to me just a fraction, speaking in what was clearly meant to be a reassuring murmur. "Look, miss, I know you're frightened. But you don't have to worry about a thing. We're going to see to it that these men don't get the chance—"

I interrupted him.

Boyd and his companion probably meant well. But being spoken to as though I were the same age as the child Rosie—simply because I happened to be female—was high on my list of experiences I particularly disliked.

"It's a supremely bad idea because you don't have the element of surprise," I said. "Those men are standing a good fifteen feet away from us. They're going to see you coming the instant you try to move from where you are now. And they're all armed. Back in America, we have a saying about not bringing a knife to a gunfight? You don't even have *knives*."

The two men exchanged another look. Then Boyd said, "Now, look, miss, you just leave worrying about all that to us."

The German speaker stepped towards our group. "Now," he said. "If you will all remain calm, there is no need for anyone—"

The rugby player suddenly sprang up and rushed at the gunman, his body low and poised for a tackle.

The clerk Boyd didn't move; he looked as though he had been petrified, his body stiff, eyes so wide they were almost bulging.

The second man managed about half a dozen running steps before the German raised his hand. His gun cracked, deafening in the echoing space.

For a split second, the ruddy-faced man seemed to hang motionless, suspended in the air. Then his body jerked, and he crashed to the ground. I clamped my teeth shut to hold back a gasp. Someone—I thought it was Rosie's mother—screamed.

No one moved, no one spoke. Everyone was staring at the body of the fallen man, shocked.

I felt sick to my stomach. This was an instance when I could definitely have lived without being proven right.

Even the four gunman looked shocked, I thought, as though this were an invisible line that they hadn't expected to cross. Or at least not so soon.

The man on the floor groaned feebly.

And almost in the same moment, Johnny stood up. "Look here," he said. "My father—"

Ice shot through me.

"Is a doctor," I interrupted.

I saw Johnny's eyes widen, but I kept going before he could interrupt, silently willing him to play along.

"John's father is a doctor, and he's a first-year medical student himself. Please, let him see if he can help."

I spoke to the man with the German accent, the one who seemed to be the leader. Behind the mask, I could see that his eyes were a pale, cold blue, but I couldn't read their expression.

"Please," I said again. "You don't want to be responsible for a man's death."

Actually I wasn't sure that the moral implications of murder would bother any of these men. What I wanted them to consider was how much more severe the penalty for killing a man would be if they were caught.

There was another silence that lasted four, then five painful beats of my heart.

The blue-eyed German frowned, scanning the circle of people as though searching for any sign that someone else might try a direct attack.

The clerks and customers all sat unmoving, tense and frightened. The fair-haired woman gave a smothered-sounding sob, clutching Rosie more tightly.

Finally, the German man jerked his head at me in a gesture of permission, waving at the injured man. "Go."

I crossed to kneel on the floor at the man's side. Johnny, his movements jerky and stiff-legged, followed me.

"Help me roll him over," I murmured.

Johnny's face was blanched white, but he complied, easing his hands under the wounded man's shoulders and rolling him gently onto his back.

The German watched us for a moment, then swung back to face the others.

"Now," he said. "Where is the bank manager?"

Mr. Poole turned a shade whiter still, his throat muscles jerking as he swallowed.

"I am the manager here."

Sickness lurched through me again as I caught sight of the wounded man's leg, which was saturated from his hip almost to his calf with blood. The bullet seemed to have torn into his thigh.

His skin was greenish gray, his eyes squeezed tight shut in a grimace of pain.

"You will now give me the keys to the bank vault," the German said to Mr. Poole.

Mr. Poole's hands shook. "I—"

"No one else need be hurt, if you will do exactly as I say," the German interrupted.

He didn't raise his voice, but the words still held enough quiet menace to drag a shiver through me.

"Yes, yes. Of course." Mr. Poole shifted his weight so that he could extract his bunch of keys and hand them over.

The German man took the keys, jerking his head at the two guards by the door. "Stay here on guard. Gordon, come with me."

The man who'd found Johnny and me was motionless for a moment, then startled, pivoted, and led the way out of the lobby, with the German following.

The German had just called him Gordon—which might have been slightly helpful, if it was actually his real name. But the way he had taken a moment to respond to being addressed by it told me that it was almost certainly a fake.

The man on the floor between me and Johnny groaned, his eyelids flickering.

"It's all right." I put my hand on his forehead and spoke softly. "It's all right. Just lie quiet. We're going to help you."

"*How?*" Johnny asked.

The guards at the door were focused on the bigger group of people.

Johnny spoke in a low, desperate whisper. "Lucy, what on earth? My father's not a doctor, and I'm no medical student, I have no idea—"

"Maybe not, but better they think you're an incompetent doctor-in-training than discover the truth."

"Why?" Johnny's brows knitted together. "My father could pay them more than they could ever hope to rob from here—"

"Yes, and what do you think they'll do if they find that out?" I hissed back. "The lives of all these other people won't be worth an hour's purchase if they find out that you're the Rockefeller heir and as such about five hundred times more valuable to them than anyone else in the room. They could just decide to shoot everyone so as to leave no witnesses, then kidnap you so that they can demand a ransom."

Johnny paled visibly; he obviously hadn't thought of that.

"Give me your scarf," I said.

"What? Why?" Johnny complied, though, unwinding the length of white silk from his neck and handing it over.

"Because we need to slow down the bleeding."

Blood was pooling on the floor under the wounded man, and already I thought his skin looked a shade more grayish-pale than it had just a moment before.

Rosie was whimpering, now, clutching her mother's hand. "You don't have any medical training, either," Johnny pointed out in a murmur.

"Maybe not." I shifted and half lifted the injured man's leg so that I could wind the scarf all the way around, just above the gunshot. "But I think we can safely assume that losing all the blood in your body can have consequences that are bad for your health."

I brought the two ends of the scarf up and crossed them, forming a knot. "Now, help me tighten this."

With Johnny's help, we tightened the makeshift tourniquet, which wrung another deep, agonized groan from the wounded man. But the bleeding slowed.

The man's eyes flickered open, bleary with pain and fear. "Thank you."

His voice was a cracked whisper.

"What's your name?" I asked.

He moistened dry lips. "George. George Parker." His face twisted up, more in fear, now, than pain, I thought. "My wife— she's expecting me to come home—"

"Just hold on," I told him. My hands were smeared, sticky with blood. I wiped them off on the ends of the scarf, then squeezed Mr. Parker's arm. "I promise we're going to do everything we can to make sure you get home to her."

I wasn't sure whether he heard me or not. His eyes had flickered closed.

"Lucy." Johnny still looked pale and shaken. "Lucy, he needs a hospital. At the very least an actual doctor—"

"I know. But right now, we're what he has instead. We need to—"

The doors leading out of the lobby crashed open, and Gordon and the German man strode in. The black masks still covered their faces, but I could see just from the rigidity of the German's shoulders and the way his hands clenched on the rifle he carried that he was furious.

He strode to the bank counters, hauled Mr. Poole to his feet, and planted the barrels of his gun against the bank manager's chest.

"You *lied!*" The German's voice was a snarl.

"No!" Mr. Poole's whole body shook with terror, and his eyes were flared wide enough to see the whites all the way around.

The German leaned forward, hissing the words from behind his mask. "The lock on the vault door is a *detector*. Put the keys in in the wrong order, and the whole mechanism seizes and cannot be unlocked. And you did not think to mention this to us before now?"

Mr. Poole was trembling and sweating, but all the same he made an effort to stand straight. "I have a duty to safeguard the money in the vault—with my life, if need be. If you have jammed the lock, it cannot be undone without the regulator key."

The German man shoved the gun harder against Mr. Poole's chest. "And where is this regulator key?"

Mr. Poole drew himself up. "It is not kept on the premises. Mr. Rathbone, the managing director of all London branches of the Capital and Counties banks, keeps it in his possession."

The German made a sound of frustration and rage. "I should shoot you right here!"

Mr. Poole's eyes were squeezed tight, his whole body rigid in anticipation of the shot. Sweat stood out on his upper lip.

"Wait!" I jumped up.

Startled, the German man's attention flicked to me—as did the attention of the other three armed men. The German's gun remained tight against Mr. Poole's chest, but three other weapons were leveled in my direction.

I swallowed against the dryness in my throat.

I had been aware before of my tendency to think first and only pause for due consideration after the fact. The habit had never had the potential to get me into quite as much trouble, though, as it did now.

I couldn't stand by and watch them shoot Mr. Poole—but in this moment, I had absolutely no idea what I was going to do or say to stop them.

A heavy knock sounded on the bank's main front doors.

I jumped, and the next moment, a deep, slightly adenoidal voice called out, "Hallo in there! This is the police. Open these doors!"

I shut my eyes for a moment, uncertain of whether it was relief or renewed terror that was flooding through me.

Someone must have heard and reported the sound of gunfire coming from inside the bank, and now one of the blue uniformed constables I had seen on duty around the city had come to investigate.

Several of the bank customers gasped, and the German spun to face the doorway, releasing Mr. Poole.

The bank manager exhaled, slid down the counter at his back, and landed with a thump on the floor, as if boneless. The door shook, another knock echoing through the lobby. "Open up!" The constable's shout filtered through to us again. "Open this door I say, in the name of the law!"

The German man strode across the lobby and seized hold of my arm. "Get rid of him," he snarled at me.

"What?" For an instant, I was too shocked to react.

Still gripping my arm, the masked German marched across the lobby to the front entrance. I glanced at the door guards, trying to gauge my chances if I managed to get hold of the German's weapon.

Stamp on the arch of his foot ... elbow to the solar plexus ... grab for the gun—

I couldn't give the move a better than eighty percent chance of working, though—and that was ignoring the other three men in the room, who would rush in to help the German the instant I made a move.

The German prodded me with the gun, motioning the two other door guards to step out of the way, out of the line of sight of the door.

"You will tell the police out there that there is nothing wrong, that the bank is closed for repairs," he growled.

I could have pointed out that the message would be more convincing coming from the bank manager. But then, Mr. Poole was currently sitting in a dazed heap on the floor, still ashen-faced and shaking.

One look at him, and any police constable with half a brain would be able to tell that something was wrong.

I nodded, silently running through my options for what I could say that wouldn't arouse the gunmen's suspicions, yet would alert the constable outside to the fact that the bank was in the process of being robbed and that a man had been shot and was possibly dying on the floor.

Sherlock Holmes could probably have come up with a brilliantly improvised code on the spot to convey just that; my mind was unfortunately a spinning blank.

The main entrance to the bank was inside a small vestibule at the front of the lobby. The bank counters and the circle of people in front of them were off to the right, out of the line of sight of anyone standing on the front steps. And when I glanced back, I couldn't see Johnny or the wounded George Parker, either.

The German drew back the bolts that locked the door and stepped into position to my left, where the opening door would screen him from view. "Do not try anything," he growled. "Or we will begin to shoot those people back there, one by one."

My chest tightened. I could possibly protect myself. I couldn't stop the other three gunmen from carrying out exactly that threat.

I took hold of the door and tugged it open, pasting on a polite smile. Time to see whether all my experience with acting was useful in the real world.

"I'm so sorry," I said.

The constable who stood on the bank steps outside was closing on forty, with a lined, square-jawed face beneath the brim of his blue helmet. He looked solid and dependable, with the shrewd awareness of a man who had seen his fair share of the seamier side of life while patrolling the London streets.

"I'm afraid the bank is closed for repairs," I said.

"Repairs?" The constable frowned, his eyes flicking across the bank's outer facade. "Looks all right to me."

"Inside repairs." I kept my smile firmly in place.

The constable's brows were still knitted together. "And who might you be, miss?"

I didn't have any convincing answer for him. Young women didn't typically work in banks. "I'm Mr. Poole's—the bank manager—private secretary," I said.

The constable's attention abruptly snagged, caught by something on my hand. "Looks like you've hurt yourself there, miss."

I glanced down, fear jolting through me in an icy burst as I saw the stain on my jacket sleeve. I had wiped my hands off, but in wrapping the makeshift tourniquet around George Parker's leg, I'd gotten blood smeared from the cuff almost to the elbow.

"I think I'd better come in, miss," the constable rumbled.

He started to come forwards, through the door.

The German stepped out of concealment, caught hold of me and dragged me against him, my back to his front, his arm across my throat. His voice was a ragged snarl. "Take one more step, and she and everyone else in this building dies."

The police constable's eyes flared momentarily wide with shock. However much he'd seen in the course of his duties, he'd obviously not been prepared for this.

For an instant, indecision hovered on his face. Then he stepped backward, raising his whistle to his lips and blowing a series of long, piercing blasts.

5. WATSON

Four of us—Holmes, Gregson, a young constable, and me—waited in a cramped little room on the second floor of a commercial building across Oxford Street from the bank. The room smelled musty with disuse and contained one stained wooden desk, one battered office chair, one telephone, and one window, which Holmes had immediately opened. He had led us from Great Ormond Street directly to the building and up the stairs, without explanation. Gregson appeared to understand what was going on, for upon our arrival he had immediately used the telephone to call New Scotland Yard. Holmes and I kept watch through the open window as the inspector received his instructions.

Gregson put down the receiver. "There is a police wagon on the way," he said. "The men have been authorized to carry firearms."

We had been waiting for about a half hour after Gregson's call when we saw a uniformed constable approach he door of the bank. He hesitated there for a few moments, apparently in conversation with someone inside. Then he stepped back away from the bank entrance. In the next moment we heard three shrill blasts from his whistle.

"Our call to arms, gentlemen!" Holmes sprang for the door. "Watson, wait here with the constable and, if the telephone rings, answer it. Gregson and I will return as soon as we can. Or if we need you, we shall call up to the window."

Irked at being left behind, but somewhat mollified by Holmes's instruction to keep watch, I waited by the window with the constable. I saw Holmes and Gregson emerge onto Oxford Street. I saw then in conversation with the constable who had blown his whistle. Then I saw a police wagon arrive, and Gregson directing other policemen who came on horseback and riding bicycles. These new reinforcements dismounted and fanned out, blocking traffic away from the bank entrance.

Holmes glanced up at me as he turned back towards our building, but he did not call out.

He and Gregson were back in our little room in two minutes time. Holmes said, "As you must have observed, there is a robbery in progress. A number of innocent customers have been taken as hostages. We must now telephone through to the bank and try to communicate with these brigands."

6. LUCY

I could only see a narrow slice of Oxford Street outside the bank, but at the sound of the policeman's whistle, the bustle of pedestrians stopped momentarily, heads turning in our direction.

I caught just a glimpse, too, of another uniformed figure in blue racing towards the bank from the direction of Argyll Street. Then the German man yanked me backwards, slamming the door shut and throwing the heavy bolts.

The other three armed men were staring at him.

"Campbell, what are you doing?" It was the heavyset man, Gordon, who spoke. "You heard that whistle. It'll bring every copper in the neighborhood here. And they know we're inside here. They'll be breaking down the door—"

"Shut up!" Campbell ripped the mask off his face, raking both hands through his hair. Without the mask, he looked very much as I had imagined: somewhere in his middle-thirties, with harsh, strong-boned features and a crest of close-cropped fair hair.

I couldn't imagine his name really was Campbell, any more than Gordon's was Gordon. Campbell was a Scottish name, not a German one.

Something tugged at the back of my mind at the thought of those names: a buried memory that refused to fully surface. I concentrated, but couldn't call it back.

My heart was beating painfully. If Campbell—whoever he really was—had abandoned all efforts to conceal his appearance, there was a strong chance he wasn't planning to leave anyone alive here who could testify to what he looked like.

The only slight advantage was that he had dropped his grip on me without seeming to notice.

Slowly, carefully, I started to inch myself away out of his reach.

The other two men—the ones whose names I didn't know— exchanged a look, shifting their weight uneasily from one foot to the other.

"I don't like this," one said. "An easy job, you said. Grab and gone. Now we've got police probably circling the whole building—"

"Shut *up*, I say!" Campbell rounded on them, his face flushed, suffused with fury.

His muscles were rigid, his breath sawing in and out.

Not good. Watching him, I could feel how quickly events had spiraled out of his control. First the detector lock on the bank vault, then the police—

He dragged in a breath, his jaw hardening. "Now listen to me. They won't break in here, not when we could kill all these people before they get through the doors. We could shoot that one again." He jerked the barrels of his rifle at George Parker on the floor. "He is wounded already, maybe dying. We kill him, then roll his body down the front steps to let them know we are serious. Then we demand that they stand back, not approach until we have had a chance to escape."

On the floor beside George Parker, I saw Johnny's face blanch. At least Mr. Parker was unconscious, unable to hear.

Campbell's plan wouldn't work. I knew with an ice-cold certainty that the police outside would never allow the robbers to walk away free.

But how many of the people in this room would they kill before that fact became clear to Campbell?

The blonde-haired young mother suddenly stumbled upright from her place on the floor. "Oh God." Her hands were clamped to her mouth. "Oh God, I can't ... I'm going to be sick—"

For a horrible, pulse-stopping second, I was certain that Campbell or one of the others was going to shoot her where she stood. Her daughter still sat on the floor, her mouth open in a perfect, round *O* of fear.

"Get her out of here," Campbell growled at Gordon.

Gordon caught hold of the woman's arm and dragged her out of the room. I waited, the hard, painful beats of my heart marking off the seconds, but no shot followed.

Campbell and the other two men were arguing in low, angry voices, not paying attention to me. I edged away until I could rejoin Johnny on the floor at George Parker's side.

"How is he?" I whispered.

"Not good, I don't think." Johnny looked down at Mr. Parker's face, and I felt a fresh chill at the sight of how pale his face was, his eyelids puckered and closed, his lips drawn back in a grimace of pain.

The leg wound was still bleeding—more slowly, with the tourniquet, but it was still seeping blood.

Johnny swallowed. "Though that may not matter, if they go through with what they're planning." He looked up at me. "Are *you* all right? They didn't hurt you?"

"No, I'm fine."

I was watching Rosie, who was crying silently again, her shoulders shaking. I wished I could think of a way of crossing over to her, but it would only attract the gunmen's attention.

Boyd, too, looked terrified. He kept staring at George Parker—probably thinking how close he had come to being the one lying here, bleeding all over the floor. I thought there was a shadow of guilt in his eyes, but he was also probably thanking his lucky stars that his nerve had failed him at the last moment—just in time to stop him from trying to attack the gunmen, too.

"Just keep quiet," Johnny said to me, his voice low and urgent. "Don't do anything else to challenge them or make them angry. Please, Lucy, promise me."

I nodded, though I was only half paying attention. Mr. Poole had inched himself over to Rosie's side. I had clearly not given the bank manager enough credit for courage. As I watched, he took out his pocket handkerchief and tied a few knots, fashioning it into the shape of a rabbit, which he drew, magician-style, out of his closed fist.

Rosie didn't smile, but she did stop crying as she watched. She raised a hand and rubbed at her eyes. Her clothing was immaculate: a flower-trimmed white hat that tied with ribbons under her chin and a dress of starched white linen and lace. But her fingers left a trail of dirt across her cheek when she tried to scrub the traces of tears away.

At her age, my hands had nearly always been dirty, too, from climbing trees and digging outside in the mud.

Anger ignited in my chest and burned, hot and insistent. There had to be a way of protecting all the innocent lives in here, a way of making sure that Campbell and the others didn't get the chance to harm or terrorize anyone else ever again.

Rosie's mother and Gordon appeared in the doorway. The woman looked flushed and shaky, the rapid rise and fall of her breathing visible even at a distance, but she wasn't hurt.

Gordon gave her a hard shove back towards the row of counters, and she stumbled back to her place beside her daughter, giving Mr. Poole a tremulous smile of thanks.

From somewhere deeper inside the bank, a telephone rang, shattering the tense stillness.

Several people gasped, and Campbell rounded on Mr. Poole. "What is that?"

Mr. Poole flinched back, his collar bobbing as he swallowed. "The ... the bank's telephone line. Inside my office."

The telephone rang again.

I stood up. "Let me answer it."

I was aware of Johnny staring at me in horror, his face stamped with a look that clearly said, What part of *don't do anything to challenge them* was unclear?

But I focused on Campbell, drawing a steadying breath and willing myself to speak calmly.

"That's probably the police telephoning, wanting to know who you are and what your plans are. And you need a way of getting a message to them, a way of letting them know that you want them to stop surrounding the bank. Let me talk to them, and I'll pass on anything you want me to say. They'll never hear your voice. They'll have no way of identifying you afterwards."

As I spoke, I kept my gaze locked on Campbell's. His eyes were icy blue and so expressionless that the fine hairs on the back of my neck rose.

I had seen that look in a man's eyes once before, while I was still at school: the look that said you weren't a human being, you were an object to be used and discarded at will.

I tensed against a shudder, shoving aside the memory of exactly how that earlier encounter had ended.

"The policeman at the door saw me. He saw you threaten me, he knows I have no reason to lie about what you intend," I said.

The moment seemed to stretch on interminably, the harsh shrilling of the telephone a raucous counterpoint to the drumming of blood in my ears.

"Come," Campbell ground out at last. He pointed the rifle at me, prodding me towards the door to the back. "I will tell you what to say."

7. LUCY

I let my hands shake as I stepped to the telephone cabinet inside of Mr. Poole's private office and lifted the receiver.

"Hello?" I allowed a slight quaver to creep into my voice, too.

Campbell was standing close beside me. He wasn't touching me, but I could feel the force of his gaze on me all the same, like a knifepoint at the small of my back.

He had already instructed me on what I was supposed to say. Now I wanted him to believe that I was too intimidated, too frightened to even think about passing on a message beyond the one he wanted me to convey.

The receiver buzzed. A female voice said, "Hold please," followed by a series of clicks.

"Hello." The voice that spoke in my ear was male. "This is Inspector Tobias Gregson, of Scotland Yard. Whom am I speaking to?"

I swallowed, briefly shutting my eyes and imagining myself into my part.

"My name is Lu—" I caught myself. I didn't need any of the bank robbers to know my real name. "Lucy Manette," I finished.

I had read Dickens' *A Tale of Two Cities* at school and occasionally wondered whether whoever had given me the name Lucy had been an admirer of the book's heroine. Although if so, I hadn't turned out to particularly resemble the fictional Lucy Manette's unfailingly angelic sweetness.

"I was a customer at the bank this morning. But then some men broke in and they had guns—" I let my voice rise and then break on a half-sob.

"Are you all right, miss?"

If I hadn't been playing a part, I would have asked whether Tobias Gregson wasn't the Scotland Yard trash collector rather than an inspector. Because under the circumstances, asking whether I was all right was a little like asking Mrs. Lincoln how she had enjoyed the play.

As it was, though, I drew a shuddering breath, wishing that I could manage to let a few tears gather at the corners of my eyes. I was usually quite good at crying on command for a theatrical performance, but at the moment, I was still too furious.

If not for Campbell and the other men, I wouldn't be worried about George Parker dying on the floor of the bank lobby, or Johnny Rockefeller being shot and killed, or a child's life being in danger.

If not for the bank robbery, I would by this time have gotten safety deposit box 583 open. I could right this moment have been back on the street and on my way, finally with some clue as to who I was and where I really came from in my possession.

"I'm not hurt," I said to the inspector on the other end of the phone. "But the men in here—they say that they'll shoot us all unless you let them walk out of here."

There was silence on the other end of the line, and then Inspector Gregson said, "Can you put one of these men on to talk to me?"

"No." I didn't want to give Campbell the chance to change his mind about letting me be the one to speak to the police. I sped up, letting the words come in a half-hysterical sounding rush.

"But they're very serious, they've already shot one man, and they say they'll shoot the other twelve people out in the lobby unless you give them what they want. Mr. George Parker, the man who's been shot, he's ... he's badly wounded, my friend has medical training and he said that the bullet entered Mr. Parker's *armis quattuor* and may have nicked the *custodiet et fores* artery. He also may have *salvum tergo fenestras*."

I stopped, pausing to draw a breath. I had hated nearly every moment I spent in Latin classes in school, but at the moment, I was desperately hoping I remembered enough to have gotten those words right.

Campbell had been shifting from foot to foot with increasing impatience and now took a menacing step towards me.

"All right!" The quiver in my voice was frighteningly easy to summon.

I also had to hope that Campbell *didn't* speak Latin and was even less familiar with medical terms for human anatomy than I was.

"I'm supposed to say that they want the regulator key that will open the bank vault. The managing director of the Capital and Counties Bank apparently has it. They also want a carriage and horses to be delivered to the back entrance of the bank and for the police outside to draw back. If you do that, they say that they'll let everyone go."

I stopped speaking and waited, my hand gripping the telephone receiver hard enough to leave a mark across my palm.

"Well, now." Inspector Gregson sounded like a man who was aware of being out of his depth, but was doing his best to remain calm. "That could take some time. Can I see what I can do and then telephone back to you at this number?"

I was holding the receiver a little away from my ear so that Campbell would be able to hear as well; I didn't want to give him any reason to think I might be trying to keep secrets from him.

I glanced at him now, and he jerked his head in a short nod.

"Yes," I said. "Just please, please hurry."

I heard the buzz of the connection being disconnected and set the receiver back in its cradle. I shut my eyes, letting out a long, shaky breath.

Step one was accomplished. Now I just had to hope that someone outside the bank—Tobias Gregson or someone else— had enough intelligence to understand what I had said.

8. WATSON

Inspector Gregson wrote furiously on his notepad. Then he set down the telephone. His look was grim. "The robbers want a carriage and horses brought to the rear of the bank and they demand that the police pull back from the perimeter to allow them to escape. Otherwise they will kill all the hostages. One man has already been wounded. The woman who spoke with me—a young lady, I think—gave a quite detailed description of his medical condition."

"Was she one of the robbers?"

"Assuredly not. She was talking to someone who was giving her instructions. She said her name was Miss Lucy Manette. Sounded scared to death, poor girl. Although she did let it slip that there are twelve other people and that they're all apparently being held in the lobby, under guard. And that the name of the man who's been shot is George Parker."

"That seems a substantive amount of information to have been conveyed by a scared young woman. Precisely what did she say about the wounded man?"

Gregson consulted his notes. "Some medical gibberish. She said the bullet entered Mr. Parker's *armis quattuor* and may have nicked the *custodiet et fores* artery. He also may have *salvum tergo fenestras.*"

Holmes shot me a meaningful look. "Miss Manette, whomever she may be, has a high degree of intelligence and a great deal of presence of mind. As Watson here will tell you, those Latin phrases are not anatomical terms. They are a message. In Latin, she has just told us that there are four armed gunmen inside, that they are guarding the doors, and that the windows at the back of the building ought to be safe to approach."

I saw my duty immediately. "I will go. I am not in uniform. I shall enter through one of the rear windows. If I am caught, I shall pretend to be a customer that the gang has previously overlooked."

9. LUCY

Campbell prowled around Mr. Poole's office, picking up objects and setting them down again. There was a feral, dangerous edge to his movements, a feeling of barely controlled violence that made me fight not to flinch every time he came near me.

The ticking of the clock that sat on Mr. Poole's desk sounded as loud as the beat of a drum.

Campbell glanced towards the door. He was getting tired of waiting for Inspector Gregson to call back. Another moment and he might decide to go back out into the bank lobby.

"You could offer to make a trade," I said.

Campbell's head snapped around to face me, his eyes narrowing. "What?"

I couldn't let him go back to the outer room—or anywhere else in the bank.

The other men were hired hands only, not particularly observant. If the police had actually understood my message—and if they were careful—they might be able to get by Gordon and the other two. Campbell was the one I was worried about, the one whose attention might be caught by anything even slightly out of the ordinary.

"The inspector is going to call back," I said. "To let you know whether he's succeeded in getting the vault regulator key. You could offer to trade him for it. Let, say, Mr. Parker go in exchange for his delivering the key to you."

Campbell's lips drew back. "Or I could simply threaten to shoot you and Mr. Parker both, if he does not do as I say."

"You could." I ignored the trickle of ice that slid down my spine.

I didn't know for certain what Campbell's background was. His English was good enough to make me think he'd been in this country for some time. The thick calluses on his hands and the pallor of his skin suggested to me that he might have been in prison up until a month or two ago—long enough for his hair to have grown out, but not long enough to erase the prison pallor.

Either way, he clearly knew fear and intimidation well. He *liked* making others afraid.

He also wasn't going to listen to me. I knew it with cold certainty. No matter how logical an argument I made, no matter how skilled I was at persuasion, he would see it as a point of pride not to allow me to influence his decision in any way.

I eyed the telephone cabinet. I hadn't yet had reason to make a telephone call in London, but the process was probably much the same as it was in America: lift the receiver, ask the exchange operator to connect me to the right number. Granted, I didn't know any numbers in London, but surely the operator could manage Scotland Yard.

Although that probably wasn't where Inspector Gregson had called from. I imagined he would have been called to the site of the bank robbery in progress, so he would have telephoned from one of the banks or businesses nearby.

I let my gaze travel around the room, making note of the position of furniture and ornaments. Then I stumbled, putting my hand to my forehead and catching hold of the edge of Mr. Poole's desk.

"Oh."

Campbell glowered at me. "What is it?"

"I feel quite … dizzy." I swayed, my voice wavering. "I think I might faint."

Campbell gave an exclamation of annoyance and moved towards me. I watched him from under my half-closed eyelids. Closer … closer …

His face was irritated, but not wary. As far as he was concerned, I didn't rank as any kind of threat.

I still had the hairpin in the cuff of my jacket, but I needed something heavier.

I waited until he came within arm's reach, then caught up the heavy marble pen holder from the desk and smashed it into Campbell's face.

The blow snapped his head back and he cried out, a sound of mingled shock and rage. The rifle flew out of his hands as he instinctively clamped over his bleeding nose and mouth.

Memories of another fight like this one hovered at the edges of my mind, but I held them off. I had maybe three seconds to end this. Let Campbell fight back, and we'd make enough noise to summon the others.

I drove a hard kick into his knee. He fell forwards, and I hit him in the back of the head with the heavy marble slab.

Campbell collapsed onto the floor and lay still, not even groaning.

My heart hammered as I reached to feel for the pulse in his neck. I found it, strong and steady, and shut my eyes in quick relief. Unconscious, not dead.

He was wearing a leather belt; I yanked it off him and used it to bind his wrists tightly together, then rapidly searched his pockets until I found a handkerchief and stuffed it into his mouth.

There was nothing else of interest in his pockets and nothing to identify him. Just a packet of safety matches and a small enameled case containing a sprinkling of snuff tobacco.

I got my hands under his arms and pulled, gritting my teeth as I tried to shift his limp weight. Always assuming that I survived until tomorrow morning, I was going to wake up feeling as though my arms had been yanked out of their sockets.

Pushing and tugging, I managed to cram Campbell under Mr. Poole's desk. Then I straightened, moving back towards the telephone cabinet.

The office door swung open, revealing Gordon. He was still wearing the black mask, but from the heavy-muscled bulk of him, I was sure it was Gordon, standing in the doorway.

My lungs constricted as though I were trying to breathe in hot glue instead of air.

Gordon was still holding his revolver in one hand. He looked around the office. I couldn't see his face, but I imagined him frowning.

"Where's Campbell?" he asked gruffly.

The desk completely hid Campbell's unconscious body. At least, from the view of anyone standing at the office entrance.

The rifle Campbell had dropped had landed behind the door, though if Gordon opened the door any wider, he was going to knock into the butt of the gun.

At which point, the natural thing for him to do would be to peer around the door to see whatever he'd struck.

I tried to force my pulse to settle back into a normal rhythm. "He went to go and check on the vault locks again," I said.

I held my breath as I said it, but Gordon nodded unquestioningly.

I eyed him, wondering whether I could knock him unconscious, as well. He was taller than Campbell and probably outweighed me by a good eighty or ninety pounds. But if I could get close enough without his suspicions being roused—

The telephone shrilled, making my heart skip and every nerve in my body lurch in response.

Now Inspector Gregson decided to telephone back.

"Well?" Gordon growled. "Answer it, why don't you. That's why you're here, isn't it?"

I moved stiffly to lift the receiver and lifted it.

"Hello?"

"Hold please." The briskly impersonal voice of the exchange operator sounded in my ear, and then Inspector Gregson's voice came on the line.

"Is that Miss Manette again?"

"Yes."

I shut my eyes for a quick second, silently willing Gordon not to come any further into the room or take it into his head to walk around the desk and find his leader's unconscious body. Then I turned slightly, angling so that I could keep an eye on him.

For the moment, at least, he was remaining in the doorway. But his presence effectively obliterated any thought of my getting an unguarded message to the police outside.

"I just wanted to tell you," Inspector Gregson went on, "that your message was received and understood."

My heart rate sped up again. Did that mean—

Inspector Gregson went on without a pause, not giving me more than a quick second to wonder whether that really meant he had understood the hidden meaning in my earlier words.

"Unfortunately, it's going to take awhile to get the regulator key from the bank director. He's out of town, you see," Inspector Gregson said. "And we're having to deal with his wife, who doesn't know the combination to his private safe ..."

I scarcely heard the words, taking them in with only one part of my mind. The rest of my attention was focused on Gordon.

I had only heard him speak a handful of times, but he struck me as a follower, not a leader. If Campbell and the others had been a pack of wolves or wild dogs, Gordon would be the whining, snapping dog at the lowest rung of the pack: allowed to share in the pack leader's kills, but never to initiate a fight or to make a decision on behalf of the whole group.

I squeezed the telephone receiver harder, clearing my throat.

"That's all right," I interrupted Inspector Gregson. "I have permission to say that as ... as a show of good faith, the robbers are willing to let Mr. George Parker and two of the other bank prisoners go. A woman and her little girl. They'll be coming out the front door of the bank shortly. Stay back; don't try to send anyone in. Just be ready to receive them."

There was a silence on the other end of the line, and I had the impression that Inspector Gregson was thinking, trying to understand what on earth was going on inside here. But then he said, "Understood, Miss Manette. Thank you."

10. LUCY

I hung up the telephone receiver, my hands shaking so much that it took me three tries to set it back in its cradle.

"That's what Campbell told you to say?" Gordon's voice was incredulous.

If even Gordon was disbelieving, there was a strong chance that I had pushed too far and that this would never work.

He also wasn't anywhere close to coming near enough that I could try to get the gun away from him. He stood unmoving, like a man-shaped mountain, firmly planted in the office doorway.

"Yes." I squeezed my eyes shut, willing a few tears to gather.

I'd learned a long time ago that the most crucial part of knowing how to fight was having a completely unbiased view of one's own strengths and weaknesses. However fast, however good I was in hand-to-hand fighting, I would never be able to match a man like Gordon in strength.

Just like Campbell, though, he would almost certainly underestimate me.

"He wrote it all down for me. See?" I caught up the upper-most paper on Mr. Poole's desk, holding it up for Gordon to inspect.

I let my voice shake as though I were on the verge of dissolving into sobs. "Campbell told me to read the words *exactly* as he had written them. He said that if I didn't, he would kill me." Gordon didn't blink an eye at the statement; apparently, that sounded more like Campbell.

His eyes moved across the page I was holding—which at a glance seemed to be a letter from a bank customer complaining about an imbalance in their account.

Then he nodded, stepping back and jerking his head for me to go out ahead of him through the door.

"Come on, then."

Relief swept through me, so intense that for a moment I genuinely *was* dizzy. I steadied myself on the edge of the desk, ordering myself not to even glance at the floor behind it to make sure that Campbell was still hidden.

Then I walked out of the room with Gordon following behind.

* * *

"You did *what*?" Johnny whispered inaudibly.

"I showed him a letter from a bank customer," I murmured back. "I thought the odds were reasonably certain that a man like him wouldn't be able to read."

We were crouched on either side of George Parker, making him as ready as we could for him to be carried out of the bank. His eyelids flickered, and he had murmured unintelligibly when I tightened the tourniquet on his leg, but otherwise he seemed still insensible, his face deathly pale.

"But what if he hadn't been?" Johnny hissed back. "What if he'd found out you were just bluffing?"

There hadn't even been time for me to give Johnny the full story. He would probably be still more horrified when he heard about Campbell.

"Then that would have been bad. But he didn't," I whispered.

On the other side of the bank lobby, Gordon was standing over Rosie and her mother, probably telling them that they were being let go. Rosie's eyes were huge and frightened as she stared up at the big man, her lower lip quivering. Her mother looked blank, as though she could scarcely comprehend what he was saying.

Tension twisted through me, stretching my nerves and coiling under my ribcage.

The other two gunmen—those whose names I didn't know— were still planted on either side of the door. But how long did we have before someone noticed that Campbell had been gone longer than he ought and went to check down in the bank vaults for him?

How long until the other gunmen searched the rest of the bank and discovered him, bound and unconscious, underneath Mr. Poole's desk?

"Ready?" Gordon loomed over us, trailed by the blonde woman and Rosie.

Johnny's expression was taut, but he nodded. "Yes. I'll need some help to carry him out of here, though. I don't want to risk jarring his injuries more than we can help."

"I can help." The voice spoke from behind us and, turning, I saw that it was Boyd, the bank clerk who had suggested the initial attack.

As we all looked at him, he swallowed visibly, passing a finger around the edge of his collar as though finding it suddenly too tight. "I mean, I'll help carry him, if you like."

There was a pause during which I counted four, then five beats of my heart, and then Gordon made an impatient *go ahead* gesture.

"Fine. Get on with it."

Boyd climbed to his feet jerkily and came over to us. "I'll take his feet," he told Johnny.

"Thanks."

Boyd wiped his forehead on the cuff of his sleeve, looking down at Mr. Parker's bloodied leg with a sickly expression on his doughy face. "Well, it's the least I can do. I mean, if I hadn't—" His throat bobbed up and down.

He and Johnny hoisted Mr. Parker up between them, the movement wringing a groan from the wounded man.

"Set him down on the front steps," Gordon ground out. "Then step back into the bank. No funny business."

Johnny and Boyd nodded and started to carry Mr. Parker towards the door. Gordon followed, his revolver held at the ready. Rosie and her mother trailed behind.

I stayed where I was, curling my hands into my palms and wishing that I could walk with them. But I also needed for Gordon and the others to go right on underestimating me, and for that to work I couldn't draw more attention to myself than I already had.

My stomach was churning, though. Not just with nerves. I couldn't manage to break free from the feeling that something was wrong, that I had missed something or overlooked something, or failed to account for some factor in this already shaky plan.

Rosie and her mother walked by me, and I winked at her, forcing a smile. She gave me the tiniest of smiles in return.

The two men by the door stepped aside, allowing Johnny and Boyd to carry George Parker through. I risked edging forwards until I could see into the small vestibule. As I watched, Gordon swung the bank's front door open, turned, and motioned for Rosie and her mother to go first.

They stepped through the door.

In the street beyond, I could see a ring of figures in blue police uniforms forming a semi-circle around the front of the bank. They must have blocked off the traffic, too, because no carriages or carts rumbled past.

Rosie and her mother walked down the bank steps. Johnny and Boyd moved sideways, awkwardly maneuvering Mr. Parker's limp form through the doorway.

I saw Gordon lean forwards, probably to issue another threat, though he kept out of the way of the open door. He wasn't entirely stupid; he must be expecting that the police outside would also be armed with guns.

Johnny and Boyd bent, lowering the wounded man down onto the bank's front stoop. I held my breath.

Johnny straightened. And Boyd leapt to his feet and bolted, launching himself down the bank steps and out into the street beyond.

11. LUCY

It took Gordon a moment longer to realize that Boyd was escaping. But then he let out a roar of rage, dove forwards, and fired his revolver at the fleeing man. The shot missed; Boyd didn't stumble or fall. But I saw one or two of the police outside raise their weapons and return fire. My heart lurched as I saw Johnny throw himself backwards, staying low to the ground and trying to protect George.

"Hold!"

I couldn't identify the owner of the voice that bellowed the word from outside. There were men standing behind the wall of uniformed police, and I thought it might be one of them, but they were too far away to see clearly.

"Unless you wish to provoke a massacre, you will hold your fire!"

Whoever it was seemed to have some authority; the gunfire stopped. Gordon bent, hauling Johnny roughly inside and leaving Mr. Parker where he was.

The other two gunmen banged the front doors shut, throwing the bolts behind them.

I took a painfully shallow breath, not daring to move. Johnny's gaze found mine. He was white, his lips pressed tight together, but he didn't look as though he had any blood on him.

"That—" Gordon began. He let out a string of obscenities that I took to refer to Boyd.

I wouldn't have expected ever to find my own opinion aligning with Gordon's—but in this case, I was in complete agreement.

Boyd hadn't just risked Johnny and George's lives by bolting. He'd endangered all of us.

Gordon's black mask still covered his face, but his whole body shook with rage. He was on the verge of snapping.

"I ought to—" He swung the gun in the direction of the group on the floor, his hand clenching and unclenching on the grip. Several of the bank customers gasped, flinching back.

I looked from Gordon to the other gunmen, my mind racing.

I needed a way to stop him, to end this without any of the other customers being hurt. But I couldn't come up with any. At best, I could make myself a target, hoping to detract attention from the others.

Maybe I *should*.

The thought seemed to come from somewhere in the deepest, most buried part of my mind, shocking in its clarity.

I didn't want to die here today. But then, Mr. Poole and all the other bank customers and clerks … they almost certainly had families waiting for them back at wherever their homes might be. Families who had no idea of the danger their loved ones were in right now, or of the holes that would be ripped in their lives if Gordon and the others shot someone they cared for.

I shut my eyes, hearing the agonized worry in George Parker's voice when he spoke of his wife, expecting him to come home.

I didn't even have a home, much less anyone who would be devastated to hear I had died. I had friends and acquaintances, many of them. But no one whose whole happiness depended on my surviving today.

That was *why* I knew how to knock a man unconscious in under three seconds. I had known from the time I was still wearing my hair in pigtails that I had to be strong enough to take care of myself. No one else was going to do it for me.

A crash, as of glass breaking, came from somewhere deeper inside the bank. Gordon spun towards the sound, his posture rigid.

"Go!" he barked at the other two men.

I shut my eyes, frustration warring with relief. This had to be a result of the message I had passed to Inspector Gregson about the windows being unguarded. Although either the police outside were outrageously inept, or else something had gone so wrong that they'd managed to effectively announce their coming by smashing a pane of glass.

The other two gunmen charged out of the room, banging the doors behind them. Gordon's shoulders were still taut, but at least he had stopped aiming the gun at the terrified group on the floor.

Are you all right? I still didn't dare move, but I mouthed the words silently to Johnny.

He ran a shaky hand across his face, but jerked his head in a quick nod.

Outside, I had to hope that Mr. Parker was being seen by a doctor—a *genuinely* trained medical professional—and soon.

Only Gordon remained inside the bank lobby. If he turned his back on me, there was a chance—

Before I could do more than calculate possible angles of attack, though, the other two gunmen were back, breathing hard. "Window's broken," one of them gasped. It was the first time I had heard him speak. His voice was nasally, slightly high-pitched for a man's. "No one in sight, but someone must have got inside, because we found Campbell. Beaten unconscious and tied up."

I breathed out silently, changing my mind about whoever had tried to get through that window. If it kept the gunmen from suspecting that I'd been the one to stow the unconscious leader under Mr. Poole's desk, then the anonymous glass-breaker had my heartiest thanks.

Johnny was staring at me, his eyes wide.

Apparently not *quite* everyone was unsuspecting of the truth.

Behind the mask, Gordon gulped in a ragged breath of air. I could almost feel the panic rolling off him. He hadn't signed on for this—for any of this—and now he was snared by circumstances beyond his control.

That only made him more dangerous, though: a dog with its leg caught in the jaws of a hunter's trap, ready to bite anyone who came near.

"I'm not doing this. We're getting out of here," he said. "Stewart, you and I are going down to the vault. Hamilton, stay here on guard. Shoot anyone who tries to get away."

12. WATSON

When the gunshot rang out, I was on my hands and knees on the ledge outside the rear window of the bank, preparing to maneuver myself inside. The shot took me by surprise. I stiffened at the sound, and the leg muscles around my old war wound rebelled from the strain of the awkward position, choosing that particular moment to go into spasm. The cramp was overpowering. I fell away from the ledge.

Worse, as I flailed about, struggling to right myself, my trailing leg struck the windowpane. I hit the ground with a painful blow to my shoulder, but stronger than the physical pain was the sting of defeat. The sound of the glass shattering would have alerted everyone inside to the intrusion. There was no chance of returning through the window. I had failed utterly.

Chagrined, I made my way back from the alley to Oxford Street. There was no time to berate myself for my ineptness, however.

Holmes was there, crouched over a wounded man. A few yards away, a blonde-haired woman and her daughter stood watching.

Holmes saw me. "Over here, Doctor! This man needs your attention."

13. LUCY

Hamilton was—to judge by his posture—one part angry and three parts terrified.

He waved the gun in Johnny's and my direction. "Sit down! There—with the others."

Johnny and I moved to rejoin the circle on the ground.

"Someone knocked Campbell unconscious?" Johnny murmured soundlessly. "You wouldn't have any idea who that can have been, would you?"

"As far as everyone in this bank is concerned, it was someone who got in from outside."

Hamilton was pacing back and forth in front of our group, from time to time glancing up nervously at either the front door or the one through which Stuart and Gordon had vanished.

Stuart, Gordon, and Hamilton. Something tugged at my memory again, a nagging tickle at the back of my thoughts. Something from years ago ... a memory from school?

Johnny leaned in a fraction closer. "What do you think they're going to do?"

"Gordon must think they can make another attempt on the bank vault door," I whispered back. "Though without the regulator key, I don't know how he thinks he can—"

I stopped speaking abruptly.

Realization had just struck me with the force of a sledgehammer blow, making the breath snag in my chest.

"What?" Johnny asked. He looked at me in alarm.

"We need to get everyone out of here," I murmured. My insides had knotted into a cold, painful clump.

Johnny eyed me, looking as though he was wondering whether the strain of the past hour had affected my mind.

"Lucy, God knows I'm not arguing," he began. "But—"

"They're going to use dynamite," I said under my breath. "Campbell had a book of safety matches in his pocket—that, and snuff tobacco. No cigarettes or cigars or anything you would need a match to light. I believe he was expecting to light a fuse."

I stared straight ahead, feeling the pieces slide together inside my mind. Gordon, Stuart, Campbell, and Hamilton.

I knew, now, where I'd heard those names before.

"But if I'm not mistaken, something is going to go wrong when they try to set off the charge of dynamite," I murmured soundlessly to Johnny. "There's going to be an explosion that kills the gunmen—and possibly us, too, if it's strong enough to make the building cave in."

Johnny was still staring at me, shocked disbelief widening his eyes. "Lucy, how do you know all of this?"

"Because Campbell and Gordon and the others—those were the names of members of Mary Queen of Scots Privy Council."

Johnny looked even more disbelieving. He gave a slight shake of his head. "Lucy—"

I stopped him, putting a hand on his wrist. "There isn't time for me to explain everything now. Do you trust me?"

I could see the struggle taking place behind Johnny's eyes, but he gulped a breath and nodded.

"Good." I squeezed his hand. "Then here's what I need you to do."

14. WATSON

I staunched the wound of Mr. Parker and bandaged it with a cotton pad and cloth one of the constables had brought from the police wagon. Then I noticed the little girl beside the blonde-haired woman looking at me. She had been crying, and her grimy hands had smeared her cheeks where she had wiped the tears away.

I looked past her, at her mother. The blonde-haired woman was staring, not at me, but at Holmes. He was standing with Gregson on the other side of the street, the two of them flanking the bank entrance, each trying to see into the window.

Then something made him turn towards the woman. I am sure their eyes met, for the look on Holmes's face was that of a tiger about to spring on its prey.

"Grab her, Doctor!" he called. "Don't let her escape!"

The woman turned, dashed the few paces to the stack of bicycles left by the constables, picked one up, and climbed on.

I took a step towards the other bicycles and nearly fell, as my right leg cramped up again.

Beside the bicycles, two of the horses of the mounted patrolmen stood tethered and waiting.

Five short words arose in my mind, resonating and irresistible, as if The Almighty had spoken them.

Your left leg is sound.

Untethering the nearest horse, I placed my left foot into the stirrup and swung myself up.

15. LUCY

"Lucy." Johnny's whisper was urgent, his expression tight. "I'm not sure I can do this, I'm not much of an actor—"

Hamilton had wandered over towards the front door, leaning in as though he were trying to hear what was happening on the street outside. He still had his gun at the ready, but for the moment, he was paying only negligible attention to us.

"You'll be all right," I told Johnny. I tried to inject every scrap of confidence I could into the murmured words. "All you have to do is follow my lead."

"Right." Johnny raked a hand through his hair. He looked far from convinced, but straightened his shoulders. "Now?"

"We need to hurry."

Gordon and the others would be rushing, too—and Campbell could regain consciousness at any second.

I swallowed. I wasn't entirely sure what one could offer an omnipotent being, but at the moment I was willing to beg God for any favors my not-wholly-exemplary life had earned in exchange for *not* letting my plan be the cause of Johnny's death.

He could die just as easily, though, if I didn't find a way to get us all out of here.

I took a steadying breath and jumped to my feet, glaring down at Johnny. "You're breaking off our engagement *now*?"

Johnny blinked at me. "Don't ... don't act as though this is a surprise."

He really *was* a terrible actor. The words came out so flat he could have been reciting the multiplication tables.

"After what's happened today, I feel I have to be honest— starting right now," he went on in the same stilted tone.

I summoned up a cry of outrage. It wasn't difficult; if I could, I would kick this entire *day* in the teeth and then trample on its remains.

"How *could* you?"

The rest of the bank clerks and customers had turned to stare at us, with looks that varied between shocked, curious, and frightened.

Hamilton spun around from the door and strode across the lobby. "Quiet!" he barked.

I turned to him, taking a few steps out of the group. "You don't understand. We were going to be *married*."

I let my voice break on a wail, covering my face but watching him through the gaps in my fingers. He had jerked instinctively backwards, and beneath the mask, I imagined his face twisting into the typical expression of panicked distaste that most men wore when confronted by a hysterical female.

I just had to hope he would be thrown off his stride enough that he wouldn't choose to shoot me where I stood.

"And now he says he doesn't want to marry me after all!"

The gunman shifted his weight uncomfortably. "Look, you've got to shut it," he growled.

The gunman was focused on me, not on the rest of the people behind me. I had been carefully angling my body so that he was forced to turn away from them in order to keep his gaze on me. Now I saw Johnny start to edge his way sideways, staying on the floor but moving into place behind Hamilton.

The gunman jerked his weapon at me, starting to gesture towards the bank counters. "Just sit back down—"

I couldn't let his attention veer away from me. The second he turned, he would see Johnny.

My heart hammered, but I kept my voice pitched at a plaintive wail. "He says he won't marry me because he's fallen in love with my grandmother!"

Hamilton looked at me, blinking behind the mask—and Johnny sprang up and struck him in the back of the head.

It wasn't an expert blow, but it was enough to make the gunman topple forwards towards me, loosening his grip on the weapon.

I caught the revolver out of his hand, seized hold of his wrist, and yanked him forwards, using his momentum to drag him off balance and down. I spun, elbowed him hard in the throat, then delivered a sharp blow to the side of his head with the butt of the gun.

Hamilton collapsed onto the floor with a faint moan.

The other hostages were staring at Johnny and me, their faces frozen in shocked astonishment.

I kept hold of the revolver in case Hamilton got up—or one of the other gunmen came back in—and spoke quickly.

"Hurry. Everyone up and to the doors, we need to get out of here. *Now!*"

There was some pushing and shoving as the shock wore off enough for everyone to jump up and race for the bank's main entrance. Johnny and I worked together, shepherding everyone through until we were the only ones who remained in the small vestibule.

Outside on the street, I could hear shouts and a general uproar—the police, no doubt wondering what was happening and why the hostages were being suddenly set free.

I glanced backwards over my shoulder, hesitating.

"What is it?" Johnny asked. "Lucy, I thought you said that we need to—"

"I know." If I was right, we needed to leave immediately. But I was thinking of the bank safety deposit box number 538, the box owned by whoever had been paying for my education all of these years.

It would probably be reckless to the point of insanity to go back into the bank now, but this might be my only chance—

A deafening roar of an explosion came from somewhere inside the bank, followed almost immediately after by a second blast, sounding much closer than the first. The whole building shook, plaster crashing down from the ceiling to fill the air with dust.

I caught hold of Johnny's hand, and we stumbled out through the front door and into the outside world of Oxford Street beyond.

16. LUCY

"Now, miss, just calm down," the police constable said. "You've had a nasty shock, and you need—"

I ground my teeth together. This was the third time the constable—it was the big, solid-looking one who had first come to the bank's front door—had given me a variation on this same speech.

I had the distinct feeling that if he'd had a cup of tea to offer me and a blanket to drape around my shoulders, he would have done it. Which was kind, but at the moment, entirely unhelpful.

"No, what I *need* is for you to listen to me," I told him.

The scene all around us was one of only marginally controlled chaos: police going from person to person amongst the newly freed bank hostages, checking for injuries. Other officers were beginning to filter cautiously inside the bank, judging whether it was safe for them to venture further in for a complete search of the premises.

All around, outside the makeshift barrier formed by the police and their vehicles, passersby were stopping to gawk and shout out questions, all summoned by the roar of the explosion.

I couldn't see George Parker anywhere—or Rosie and her mother, either.

Johnny came over to stand beside me, addressing the police constable. "My name's Rockefeller," he said. "John Davison Rockefeller Jr. I think, Constable—" Johnny paused.

"Cook, sir." The policeman's eyes widened slightly at mention of Johnny's name.

"Very well, Constable Cook. I think you had better listen to what this lady has to say."

The constable nodded, his expression respectful beneath the brim of his domed blue helmet. "Yes, sir."

I drew in a breath. I didn't have time to be annoyed that I couldn't get the constable to listen to two words while Johnny commanded instant attention. The matter was too urgent for that.

"Did any of the bank robbers inside survive?"

"Doesn't look like it." Constable Cook glanced at the building behind us. "First reports are that they blew themselves up. Must have made a mistake with the dynamite charge. Tricky stuff, explosives. Not something you want to tangle with unless you know what you're doing."

I heard Johnny pull in a quick breath and look at me sharply, but I kept going.

"It wasn't a mistake. Someone deliberately gave them faulty explosives, ones that must have been engineered to detonate early."

Constable Cook's eyebrows shot up.

I locked my hands tight together and went on, trying to choose my words with care. Everything was perfectly clear and plain inside my own mind—but I had never been more aware that what made complete sense to me often struck other people as borderline outrageous.

"The men who took us hostage, who seemed to be executing the robbery, they weren't working alone," I said. "They didn't know that the lock on the bank vault was a detector and that they would need a regulator key once they tried to force it open. Obviously, they weren't fully prepared with all the details the job entailed. I believe they were acting on orders—orders from someone who was keeping them at least partially in the dark. Campbell seemed to be the leader of the gunmen inside. But there were one or two moments when he seemed to wait before making a decision—as though he were taking orders from someone, someone who didn't want their role to be known, but who was giving him covert signals."

That was logical, but also sounded tenuous, I knew, so I kept going, scanning the crowded street as I spoke.

Mr. Poole was standing with Boyd, the runaway clerk. Boyd was clutching his nose, his eyes watering in a way that made me suspect that his face had just had a violent encounter with Mr. Poole's fist.

The bank manager was breathing hard, his formerly immaculate mustache turned into a bristling bottle-brush. I imagined that Boyd's odds of remaining an employee of the Capital and Counties Bank had just plummeted into the negative-numbers range.

"The names that the gunmen chose to call each other—their aliases—were all chosen from history," I said. "Gordon, Hamilton, Stuart, and Campbell. I knew I'd heard those names before, but it took me until just now to remember that they were part of the privy council of Mary, Queen of Scots."

Johnny was frowning at me, looking bewildered. "You said that inside, I know. But what—"

"Mary, Queen of Scots. A *woman*," I emphasized. "I believe that a woman planned and executed all of this—and disposed of the men she had hired to carry out the dirtier parts of the job once they had served their purpose."

Johnny's mouth dropped open in shock. Constable Cook took a breath as though he were going to say something.

I spoke rapidly. "There was a woman inside the bank, one of the other customers. Or so we thought. She had a little girl with her. Apparently her daughter. Except that I don't think she really was. The child was just part of her cover identity. Who would suspect a young mother with a child?"

I hadn't suspected her myself. I had done my utmost to get Rosie and the blonde-haired woman out of the bank. Although if I hadn't intervened, I assumed the woman would have found another way to exit safely.

Constable Cook's expression turned from one of shock to wary appraisal as he eyed me. "Now, miss, I have to tell you—" he began.

"No, listen," I insisted. "She said she was feeling ill, which could be natural—everyone in the bank was sick with shock. But she just got up and left her daughter alone, with a lot of armed gunmen. No loving mother would do that. It was just a ploy—a ploy so that she could get into the back of the bank and steal whatever it was she came for. I'm not certain, but Mr. Poole mentioned a necklace worn by Queen Elizabeth I. That would fit with the Mary Queen of Scots theme."

I took a breath. "There's more. The little girl Rosie was immaculately dressed, but her hands were dirty. That could be just harmless childishness, but it made me wonder whether the clothes were really hers or just a costume that she'd been dressed up in to look the intended part of a wealthy woman's daughter."

I remembered, too, how anxious the blonde woman had been not to let Rosie speak to me. I had taken it for nervousness at the time. But maybe Rosie's accent wasn't that of an upper-class child.

"Miss—" Constable Cook said again. His cheeks were turning slightly ruddy.

"And more than that," I finished, "the gunman who was negotiating to let them and Mr. Parker go—he was very careful to keep Johnny under guard with his gun. But he actually turned his back on Rosie and her mother. That could just mean that he didn't consider her a threat—most men wouldn't. But put it together with everything else, and it *is* suggestive. At the least, you need to find this woman and see whether she really is who she claims to—"

"*Miss.*" Constable Cook's voice rose to a pitch impossible to ignore. "That's what I've been trying to tell you. We're already going after the woman."

I blinked. "You are?"

Constable Cook's annoyance faded, to be replaced by a look of puzzlement. "That's right, miss. It's the most extraordinary thing, but Mr.—" He stopped, clearing his throat. "Well, never mind that. Someone else said that very same thing you did—about the little girl's hands being dirty and about it not matching the rest of her. He took it to Inspector Gregson, but by that time the woman had done a bunk and vanished. Mr.—that is, the gentleman I mentioned before and Inspector Gregson went after her. We're just waiting for word as to whether they catch her."

I frowned. "Who exactly is this gentleman?"

Constable Cook's face flushed an even deeper shade of crimson. He stared fixedly down at the toes of his sturdy boots.

"Sorry, miss, can't say. Just someone who occasionally helps the police with their inquiries."

17. WATSON

I had heard the great roar of an explosion and then another. My one thought was to stay abreast of the fleeing female cyclist and prevent her from getting off and running into one of the buildings. However, she seemed to have a different plan. She appeared to be trying to get as far away as possible as quickly as possible, and I could not have that either. I had to keep her contained so that the police could capture her. I knew that if we both were on the ground, I with my hampered leg would be at a disadvantage.

Holding myself in the saddle, fortunately, had not caused my old wound to spasm once more. As we came to the nearest intersection off Oxford Street, I urged my horse up and in front of her, herding her onto the cross street, forcing her to turn. I did the same at the next intersection. There I saw Holmes and Gregson, about to climb aboard the police wagon.

The woman saw them too of course. She veered off to one side.

But as she sped past the wagon, pedaling furiously, Holmes was ready for her. He had reached into the wagon and emerged brandishing a patrolman's baton.

With one deft thrust, he leaned out and inserted the baton between the spokes of the blonde woman's front bicycle wheel. The results were spectacular. The front wheel locked and the bicycle pitched forward, throwing her over the handlebars. She twisted, crashing into the side of the police wagon. At the impact, her blonde wig came off, flying onward for a few yards before landing in the dust of the road.

Now revealed as a brunette, she sprawled against the wagon wheel. Then she got her feet under her and stood.

Turning, she faced Holmes, Gregson, and two uniformed constables. Though it was plainly impossible for her to escape, she appeared undaunted.

Chin outthrust, head erect, she wiped the dust from her face and straightened her straggly hair.

"It's Sherlock Holmes, isn't it?" she said. "So you're not dead after all, are you? Worse luck."

Holmes ignored this. "Gentlemen, let me introduce you to Lillie Martin, known in some circles as Lillie the Lift, Lillie the Lure, or, in one recent instance, 'Killer Lillie.'"

The woman glared at Holmes, her features twisted. She spoke in a sullen snarl. "They never proved that."

"But this time they will. The landlady across the street from Mrs. Palfrey's will identify you. The pub man or the waitress in The Swan will identify you. Someone may even recall your recommending the coca nerve lozenges to the unfortunate Mr. Palfrey. And even if they do not, you will have your employer to reckon with for the deaths of several of his hirelings—hired by or through you, doubtlessly, to protect his identity. The word will get about that five men connected to one of his enterprises died in vain. That will do little for his reputation as a successful criminal mastermind. I doubt he will provide you with the same legal talent as he has sent forth to defend you for the past crimes you have committed in his service."

She gave a sly grin and made an airy gesture with her hand. "I'm sure I don't know wot yer talkin' about."

"How many long nights did you have to spend beguiling Simon Palfrey? You needed him to bring you the wax impression of the key to his brother's locker at the bank, from which you could extract the keys to the safety deposit boxes. But once he had done that—two Sundays ago, I would expect—he was expendable."

"'E was a fool, I'll say that much."

"More than that, he was a liability, for he could identify you when his bank investigated, as they inevitably would following the robbery."

"But he won't be doin' that now, will 'e?"

"Because two Sundays ago, you placed a poisoned lozenge into the box containing the coca nerve tonic tablets. You could not tell how long it would take before the poisoned lozenge came into the eager and trusting hand of Simon Palfrey, but you knew that one day it would. So you took the room across the street and waited. I saw you at your window when I stood over your victim this morning and removed the box of lozenges from his pocket. You knew that when the police or the doctor or the mortician arrived, it would be safe for you to act. You had the men on call, waiting to strike the within mere hours of Simon's death. But it took capital, did it not, all those preparations? This lovely dress, the outfit for the little girl, the room rent, the payment needed to keep the five accomplices available? And you did not make that investment yourself, did you?

And now your investor—your employer—will have nothing to show for his efforts, and he will extract his payment from you."

At this, Lillie's head snapped up. She stared at Holmes for a long moment. "I don't know what you mean."

"I mean the emerald, Lillie. You failed to procure the emerald."

She glared. "I have no emerald. You can search me."

"You are willing to submit to a search because you imagine that you threw the emerald to an accomplice—likely the cabman you passed—just before we stopped your mad dash on the bicycle."

"I don't know any cabman."

"But when the cabman presents the jewel to his employer—and yours—he will find that it is only a glass replica. And your employer will not be pleased. No, Lillie, he will not be pleased."

Lillie's jaw went slack. She gaped at Holmes.

He went on, his voice silken. "The emerald was a fake, Lillie. A lure, if you will. How appropriate that *you* were the one sent to take the bait."

Lillie's beady brown eyes darted back and forth, as though seeking some way out. She put both hands in her coat pockets and leaned back against the police wagon. Her voice came in a whisper. "A fake emerald."

"It was bait for a trap, to catch your employer," Holmes said. "Tell us his name and you may escape the noose."

She shook her head. Then she spat on the ground and glared at Holmes, defiant.

"There won't be no escapin' '*im*," she said.

Then in the next moment, quick as lightning, her right hand came out of her pocket. In a flash it was at her mouth. Holmes leaped forward and grasped her wrist, but it was too late. Moments later, Lillie convulsed and died in Holmes's arms. He lowered her body to the ground. "I should have anticipated that she would have poison," he said. "I should have had her cuffed."

"She never would have talked," said Gregson. "Not that one. What she just did is the proof."

He motioned to the constables to take away the body.

18. LUCY

"So. I'm in love with your grandmother, am I?" Johnny said. We were sitting side by side on the front steps of a gentleman's haberdashery shop that stood across the street from the bank.

Most of the excitement had died down. The police had roped off the entrance to the bank for safety's sake, and the majority of their carriages were drawing away. Even the gawkers were beginning to find other places to be.

Johnny and I, though, had been asked to remain, just in case Inspector Gregson had any further questions to ask us when he returned.

"Well, yes," I said. "But don't worry. I'm sure my grandmother—whoever she may be—is stunningly lovely and well worth your adoration."

My smile faded, though, as I looked across the street towards the bank. The building's outer structure was undamaged, but the vault was a total loss—and so was the safety deposit box room.

It seemed selfish, in the midst of all the death and violence that had occurred here today, to be thinking about my own reason for coming to the bank. But the fact remained that I *might* have a grandmother alive somewhere. And I had just watched my best chance at finding her—or any other clues to my origins—explode right along with the charges of dynamite.

"You'll find out what you want to know someday," Johnny said. "I've never met anyone more determined than you."

"Thank you."

"Lucy—" Johnny began.

I interrupted. "Look!"

A uniformed police constable was approaching, carrying Rosie in one arm. I drew in a breath of relief at the sight of her.

The little girl's flower-trimmed hat had been knocked askew, and she was dusty, but seemed otherwise unharmed.

I jumped up and crossed over to the constable. "Excuse me." He turned.

"Is she all right?" I asked.

The constable nodded. "Found her dumped by the side of the road a few streets over from here, poor kid," he said. "But she's not hurt."

He set Rosie on the ground, and I crouched down in front of her.

"Can you tell us what happened?" I asked her gently.

Rosie's eyes were big and scared looking, but she nodded. "The lady saw me playing kick-the-can in the street and said she'd give me a whole ten shillings if I came with her and acted like I was her daughter." Now that she was allowed to speak freely, I could hear the tones of East London in her small, high-pitched voice. "But she never said nothing about guns and all those nasty men and all of that."

She cast a quick, worried look at the policemen, her lower lip beginning to tremble. "Am I in trouble? Am I going to jail?"

"No, of course not." I squeezed her hand. "You haven't done anything wrong. Where do you live? Do you have any parents?"

Rosie nodded. "My dad's a sailor. He's away at sea now. My mum's gone to work in the matchstick factory while he's gone, because we couldn't pay the rent." Her chin wobbled again. "She'll be worried about me if I'm not there when she comes home."

"We'll make sure you get back to her safely," I told her. I straightened, addressing the constable. "Would that be all right? Mr. Rockefeller here and I can see that she gets back to where she belongs. We can get the address in case you need it for the official police reports, but I can't imagine anyone will need to speak with her again. She won't be able to tell any more than what she already has."

The constable hesitated, looking from me to Johnny, but then nodded. Probably because the Rockefeller name had done the trick once again.

"I suppose that would be all right. Come along, young missy." He held out a hand to Rosie. "We'll go and find a carriage for the nice lady and gentleman to drive you home in."

"A drive in a *carriage*? Really?" Rosie's whole face brightened, all thoughts of tears forgotten. She'd probably never ridden in a carriage before in her young life.

As well as seeing her home, I would also make sure that Johnny gave her mother a check large enough that they would have no further worries about paying the rent. Not that I expected Johnny to argue or resist.

A middle-aged man with brown hair and a harried expression approached, caught sight of Johnny, and quickened his steps. "Mr. Rockefeller!"

Mr. Foster was a security specialist hired by Johnny's father to protect Johnny while he was in England. His duties included making arrangements for some of the Rockefellers' upcoming business meetings as well, which was why he hadn't accompanied us to the bank today. But at the moment, he was clearly imagining what would have happened if he had to inform Mr. Rockefeller, Senior that his only son and heir had been killed in a bank robbery.

"Good heavens." Mr. Foster mopped his brow. "You said that you would be here, and when I arrived and saw the police—" He shook his head, swallowing visibly. "When your father learns of this narrow escape—"

Johnny smiled, clapping Mr. Foster on the shoulder. "As far as I'm concerned, this entire morning can be chalked up under the heading of *what my father doesn't know, won't hurt him.*"

Mr. Foster looked at him, his conscience clearly waging war with his sense of self-preservation. "But I was hired by your father—"

"To see that I came to no harm. Which I haven't," Johnny said. "In light of that, I think we can all pretend that Lucy and I were nowhere near Oxford Street today. In fact, I believe we carried out our plan to see—what was it, Lucy?"

"The Tower of London. I've always wanted to see the famous ravens."

"There you are." Johnny clapped Mr. Foster on the back again. "My name might appear in the police reports—I told one of the constables who I am. And I also gave my name to the bank manager, a fellow named Poole. But I expect you can arrange for both of them to conveniently forget that, can't you, Foster?"

Mr. Foster looked at him a long moment, then nodded slowly. "Yes, Mr. Rockefeller. I hope you and the young lady enjoyed your visit to the Tower."

He moved off.

"Poor old Foster." Johnny shook his head "He must have had heart failure when he learned I was actually inside the bank while it was being robbed."

"Will he get into trouble?" I asked.

"Not if we all agree to tell no one."

"I won't say anything. As far as I'm concerned, you can scratch the visit to the Tower and just tell anyone who asks that you haven't even seen me while you've been in London."

I looked up at Johnny. "Thank you for everything you did back there inside the bank today, though. You were very brave."

"Not as much as you. You were … astonishing." Johnny shook his head, looking at me with an unaccustomedly serious, almost nervous cast to his gaze. "Lucy, if you wanted—" He cleared his throat. "I mean to say, if you like, I could make an effort at fireworks or—what was the other thing?"

"Hot air balloons."

"Yes, that."

I met Johnny's gaze, something sharp twisting inside me. I felt oddly closer to taking Johnny's proposals seriously— closer to *accepting* his proposal—than I ever had before. Not because I had changed how I felt about him. I liked Johnny very much, just the same as I always had.

But I was thinking about that moment inside the bank, when I realized that no one was waiting for me outside the bank, no family to miss me if I were gone or be overwhelmingly thankful for my safe return.

It would be nice to have someone I fit with, somewhere I belonged.

But then, wherever that was, it wasn't in Johnny's gilded world of influence and etiquette and power. I'd always known that, and it wasn't going to change. And Johnny ... I knew just as surely that he liked the idea of me—but he didn't really know or understand me, not fully.

I leaned forward so that I could kiss his cheek. "I would make a terrible princess," I said. I smiled at him. "But thank you. I'm glad that we're friends."

There was a shadow that might have been sadness in Johnny's gaze, but he returned the smile.

"So am I, Lucy James."

I looked past him, towards the soot-tarnished outline of the Capital and Counties Bank, and wished, just for a moment, that I knew who it was who had interpreted my coded message, who it was who had noticed Rosie's dirt-smudged hands. I wanted to know that almost as much as I wished I knew the origins of my own name.

But then—especially in a city the size of London—it was spectacularly unlikely that I would ever discover that or find the mysterious person again.

I took Johnny's arm.

All around us, the bustle of Oxford Street was resuming as though it had never been interrupted: wagons and carriages of every size and description rattling along the cobbled streets, flower vendors and vegetable cart sellers hawking their wares, newspaper boys crying out the latest headlines on the corners. A troop of acrobats had set up camp across from a knife-grinder's stall on the corner and were performing backflips and handsprings in front of a man's top hat set out for donations.

The whole scene seemed to hum with the fierce rush of London life, echoing through me almost like the beat of a second pulse. I might not have a home, but there was liberty in that; it meant that I was free to choose my own path, carve out for myself whatever space I wanted to occupy in the world.

I could make London my home. Despite our somewhat rocky and unorthodox introduction, I loved the great city—the Great Cesspool, as Dr. Watson had famously described it already.

"Come along," I told Johnny. "Let's take Rosie back home."

19. WATSON

"Ultimately a sad case, Watson," Holmes said, shortly after we returned to our rooms on Baker Street. "Although it gave evidence of some of the finest traits in human nature, it was mainly illustrative of the worst. And I blame myself."

I protested. "But you foiled a robbery. You caught Lillie Martin. And it remains possible that the police will somehow trace the cabman to whom she passed the false emerald—"

He interrupted. "You persist in featuring my successes, Watson. As you do in all your accounts of our adventures. Yet in this case I am at fault, for I badly underestimated the evil in the heart of my opponent."

"Miss Martin?"

"No, Watson. The primary evil lies in the criminal mastermind, the person whose identity I had hoped to learn. He was more malevolent than I had anticipated. He chose associates who had no compunctions about destroying the private property of hundreds of people, although doing so gave them no benefit. And he chose Lillie Martin, who had no compunctions about murdering those associates."

"You think she tinkered with the fuses on the dynamite?"

"She would have not had the skill. Yet she had to know that her associates would die. The plan was for her to leave the bank with the jewel. Her confederates were instructed to remain for a time, taking the opportunity to loot the bank's vault and then to bargain their way to freedom using the hostages. But they all were to perish, and Lillie Martin and her employer both knew it. You saw her face when I suggested that there might be bad consequences for her due to the deaths of the other robbers. She had no fears on that score whatsoever. It was only when I told her that the jewel was false that she lost her composure, realizing that she would have to face the consequences of failure."

"But why did the others have to die? Surely they could not identify the mastermind. Or would he have them all killed so they could not identify Miss Martin?"

"He had them killed so that there would be fewer accomplices to pay."

I drew in my breath. "That is appalling, Holmes," I said. "To betray five men—to take their lives, leave their families bereaved and forsaken—simply to increase one's ill-gotten gains. Now I see why you find the case illustrative of the worst features of human nature."

At our mantel, Holmes picked up his Persian slipper and began to fill his pipe. "We are fortunate that the deaths were limited to the criminals. But we are no further to knowing the name of identity of our adversary than we were at the onset of the scheme, when last August I disguised myself as the representative of an anonymous noble lady and brought the supposedly priceless gem to Mr. Poole at the bank."

"You did that? You astonish me, Holmes."

"You recall I had my own account at the bank and I had dealt with Mr. Poole before. I knew him to be a chatterbox, unable to keep a secret, and that he would boast of the increase in status that his office would attain by virtue of the trust placed in it for such a priceless purpose. It was only a matter of time before word of the emerald reached the criminal classes. Still, my plan failed in its primary objective."

"I have one question, Holmes. Earlier you spoke of this case as one illustrating the finer qualities of human nature."

Holmes lit up his pipe. "I was thinking of the young woman who called herself Lucy Manette. Although under great duress, she had sufficient courage and intelligence to send us the coded message. Also, Mr. Poole said he did not doubt that he owes his life to her. And Gregson said the hostages were fulsome in their praise of her heroism. It seems a pity that she left Oxford Street before we returned, for I would have liked to thank her personally."

"I agree," I said. "One cannot be entirely pessimistic about the future of our sorry old world when it has people like Miss Manette in it."

Holmes took to his chair before our fire. For a long time he gazed in silence at the glowing coals.

Then he said, "I wonder what her real name is."

THE END

HISTORICAL NOTE

Sir Arthur Conan Doyle in *The Adventure of the Priory School* identifies the Oxford Street branch of the Capital & Counties Bank the bank of Sherlock Holmes. It was, in fact, a real bank in London in the late Victorian era—although there is no record of Sherlock Holmes ever foiling a robbery attempt there.

Lucy's martial arts skills may seem like an anachronism for a young Victorian woman, but in fact have some grounding in historical fact. The women's suffrage movement, which was building momentum around the turn of the century, encouraged its members to become practiced in self-defense so that they could better resist arrest or combat police brutality during demonstrations. Many militant suffragettes became adept in an eclectic style of martial arts known as Baritsu—which coincidentally was also made famous by Sir Arthur when he identified Sherlock Holmes as a practitioner.

The Bartitsu Club in London was one of the first martial arts schools in Europe to open its classes to women. Suffragette leader Sylvia Pankhurst was quoted in the New York Times as saying,

We have not yet made ourselves a match for the police, and we have got to do it. The police know jiu-jitsu. I advise you to learn jiu-jitsu. Women should practice it as well as men.

We can only imagine that Lucy James would have approved.

A NOTE OF THANKS TO OUR READERS, AND SOME NEWS

Thank you for reading this prequel to the *Sherlock Holmes and Lucy James Mystery Series*.

If you've enjoyed the story, we would very much appreciate your going to the page where you bought the book and uploading a quick review. As you probably know, reviews make a big difference!

The next three adventures in the series are currently available in e-book, paperback and audiobook formats:

The Last Moriarty
The Wilhelm Conspiracy
Remember, Remember

Watch for more Sherlock and Lucy books to be released in 2017, including:

The Jubilee Problem (September)
Death at the Diogenes Club (November)

And next year, be sure to watch for *The Return of the Ripper* and a collection of Sherlock and Lucy short stories, coming in early 2018!

ABOUT THE AUTHORS

Anna Elliott is the author of the *Twilight of Avalon* trilogy, and *The Pride and Prejudice Chronicles*. She was delighted to lend a hand in giving the character of Lucy James her own voice, firstly because she loves Sherlock Holmes as much as her father, Charles Veley, and second because it almost never happens that someone with a dilemma shouts, "Quick, we need an author of historical fiction!" She lives in Maryland with her husband and three children.

Charles Veley is the author of the first two books in this series of fresh Sherlock Holmes adventures. He is thrilled to be contributing Dr. Watson's chapters for this and future books in the series, and delighted beyond words to be collaborating with Anna Elliott.

Made in the USA
Las Vegas, NV
22 February 2022

44385305R00066